Advance F

MW01205183

Yermiyahu Ahron Taub's collection, *Prodigal Children in the House of G-d*, is cleaved down the middle—five stories of daughters, five of sons—then sewn together by the stories themselves, which intertwine in surprising and delightful ways as characters jump from story to story and get bruised or healed in the process. Taub is a brave, exacting, and large-hearted writer who cares deeply about his characters as they question the lives they have inherited or chosen, and he passes no judgment on saints and sinners alike. Whether their ghetto is ultra-Orthodox, gay or small-town America, Taub's characters are on quests that stretch over lifetimes and are riveting to watch.

—Evan Fallenberg, author of *The Parting Gift*

Not all poets can also write prose, but Yermiyahu Ahron Taub certainly can. In a mere dozen pages or so, his story "Lettering and the Art of Living" succeeds in capturing a woman's entire lifetime, and by evoking many of her memories, feelings, and even her historical context, he awards dignity to this humble individual's solitary, not fully-lived life. "Lettering and the Art of Living", infused with a poet's sensibility and sensitivity, is an accomplished and moving story.

—Nora Gold, author of *The Dead Man*, *Fields of Exile*, and *Marrow*; and Editor of Jewish Fiction .net

Each story in Yermiyahu Ahron Taub's *Prodigal Children in the House of G-d* renders an elegant portrait of a lonely soul, confronting demands of ultra-Orthodox or other conservative tradition. Simmering with inner resistance, these characters—lesbian, hetero, gay—struggle to shape their birthrights on their own terms. Taub offers a wealth of sensitive insights into minds and hearts rarely depicted on the page.

—Daniel M. Jaffe, author of *The Genealogy of Understanding* and *Jewish Gentle* and *Other Stories of Gay-Jewish Living*

Taub's story collection addresses the gaps in understanding and faith between parents and children in a vivid, tender, and bittersweet way. People, mostly young, find themselves suddenly at odds with their previous reality, often through no fault of their own, suffering the painful fallout from what Heinrich von Kleist called "the imperfection inherent in the order of the world". And yet Taub's characters bring a quiet courage to their situations: the mother of a banished gay son reconnects with him before his death, a girl whose rabbi father has viciously dismembered her Barbies is comforted by her brother, a young girl dreams the impossible dream of becoming a scholar of the Torah. These stories are grounded in fine detail from the fussy furnishings of a boarding house to a polka-dotted half-veil hat that begins a deep friendship. This collection is at once elegiac and edgy, wise and witty, and I am certain this will be the most rewarding story collection I will read this year.

—Margaret Meyers, author of *Dislocation*

Prodigal Children in the House of G-d is a beautifully written, finely detailed, big-hearted, generous, and an intimate story collection full of fascinating daughters and sons who will stay with this reader for a long time to come. Make yourself a big pot of tea, sink down into a comfortable chair, and turn off all your devices. This is a book to spend time with, pay attention to, savor, and enjoy.

—Lesléa Newman, author of *A Letter to Harvey Milk*

The prodigal children in Yermiyahu Ahron Taub's elegant and lovely new collection are each—to paraphrase a famous Talmudic dictum—a fully individual and necessary world. They are also worlds in exile, finding dignity in often modest but gratefully free lives achieved at enormous cost. As we come to know more and more of them, they form a universe that moves us to the core. Though Taub's background may make us assume the influence of the great Yiddish writers, his characters seem more like those in the works of Mavis Gallant or Virginia Woolf had they been born into a different tradition.

—Aryeh Lev Stollman, author of *The Far Euphrates* and *The Illuminated Soul*

Photo credit: Tamar London

Yermiyahu Ahron Taub is the author of six books of poetry, including *A moyz tsvishn vakldike volkn-kratsers: geklibene Yidishe lider/A Mouse Among Tottering Skyscrapers: Selected Yiddish Poems* (2017). *Tsugreytndik zikh tsu tantsn: naye Yidishe lider/Preparing to Dance: New Yiddish songs*, a CD of nine of his Yiddish poems set to music was released on the Multikulti Project label (www.multikulti.com) in 2014.

Taub was honored by the Museum of Jewish Heritage as one of New York's best emerging Jewish artists and has been nominated four times for a Pushcart Prize and twice for a Best of the Net Award. With Ellen Cassedy, he is the recipient of the 2012 Yiddish Book Center Translation Prize for *Oedipus in Brooklyn and Other Stories* by Blume Lempel (Mandel Vilar Press and Dryad Press, 2016). Please visit his website at www.yataub.net.

For Ellen Cassedy

Yermiyahu Ahron Taub

PRODIGAL CHILDREN IN THE HOUSE OF G-D

Stories

To the McGonigle Family —

Love,

ahron

22 June 2018

Wareham, Mass.

AUSTIN MACAULEY PUBLISHERS™

LONDON • CAMBRIDGE • NEW YORK • SHARJAH

A CIP catalogue record for this title is available from the British Library.

ISBN 9781788231572 (Paperback)
ISBN 9781788231589 (E-Book)

www.austinmacauley.com

First Published (2018)
Austin Macauley Publishers Ltd™
25 Canada Square
Canary Wharf
London
E14 5LQ

Acknowledgments

I am grateful to the editors of the following publications in which these stories appeared:

Jewish Fiction .net (October 2016/Rosh Hashana 5777): "Lettering and the Art of Living"

The Jewish Literary Journal (March 2016): "Undressing After Sinai"

Jewrotica (May 9, 2016): "Angel of the Underworld"

Second Hand Stories Podcast (March 9, 2017): "Flowers for Madame"

I am grateful to the Board of Directors and staff of The Writers' Colony at Dairy Hollow (Eureka Springs, Arkansas) for a residency in autumn 2015 during which these stories were written and this book was conceived and structured. I thank director Linda Caldwell, cook and housekeeper Jana Jones, and the writers in residence at the time, including Cynthia Erb, Dot Hatfield, Judi Ketteler, Pat Couch Laster, and Laura Van Prooyen. I thank Eureka Springs residents Josh Clark and Jan Schaper.

I thank the Editorial Board of Austin Macauley Publishers for their belief in my work and staff members, including Amanda Harrison, Alexander Heightman, Kirsten Jolly, Jessica Norman, Rebecca Ponting, whose contributions enhanced the publication process.

For early words of support, I thank Evan Fallenberg, Nora Gold, Daniel M. Jaffe, Margaret Meyers, Lesléa Newman, and Aryeh Lev Stollman.

For support of various kinds, I thank Angelika Bammer, Zackary Sholem Berger, Andrew W. M. Beierle, Susana H. Case, Cindy Casey, Krysia Fisher, Ken Giese, Pearl Gluck, Elizabeth Heaney, Miriam Isaacs, Cecile Esther Kuznitz, Elizabeth Goll Lerner, Laura Levitt, Jeff Mann, Erin McGonigle, Yankl Salant, Paul Edward Schaper, Jeffrey Shandler, and Phil Tavolacci.

Ellen Cassedy has been a friend, colleague, and close reader of my work for a long time. I've learned so much from Ellen's attention to language, her writerly talents, her rigorous decision making process, and her *mentshlekhkeyt*, to name but a few of her gifts. It was Ellen who once asked me if I'd considered writing short stories. That question propelled me on the path towards this collection. And you were with me when I was laid low.

Thank you, Ellen.

Author's Note

The stories in this collection are works of fiction. Names, characters, places, and events are either the products of the author's imagination or are used fictitiously. Any resemblance to actual persons, living or deceased, or locales, is purely coincidental.

Table of Contents

I. Daughters

"Night in the Solarium"

Madame Maisie's rooming house was located to the left of the town square and served as a landmark for locals and travelers alike. It was on a busy street, and yet it was sufficiently set back to be shielded from most of the commotion. Even the clanging of the streetcar, which drove by every half hour, was only charming background noise when heard from inside the house. Papa had planted bushes, hedges and trees, even a magnolia, which also helped block out some of the street noise.

Still, all of the greenery was maintained so as not to obscure the gingerbread allure of the house, with its filigree and carving and cupolas with inset balconies painted shades of wine-red and gray. That was how Papa kept the house in his day, and that was how he urged the young(er) Maisie to preserve it when he passed on. Besides, Madame Maisie wanted the house to be visible from a distance so that it could be quickly recognized by potential lodgers on the street.

Madame Maisie knew the architecture of the rooming house was now considered old-fashioned, a remnant from a bygone era, as perhaps she herself was. If not for the intervention and clout of the Historic Preservation Society, of which Madame Maisie was a proud member, homes such as hers would have been destroyed a long time ago. Clean lines, function, simplicity, and unity with nature were the guiding principles of the current day. But she was proud of the house, not as a relic or an heirloom, but with its distinction and well-maintained grounds, as an exemplar of the good life. Furthermore, she understood that together the house and the grounds represented a balancing act of sorts; sufficient greenery for quiet and shade yet not too much so as to obscure the attraction or architectural wonder, as her father once proudly asserted, of the structure.

Madame Maisie believed that balance was the key to life, and she sought to impart this message to her lodgers in subtle and sometimes not-so-subtle ways. She also knew that the historic preservation work in the town as a whole now attracted guests, who saw the town as a site that offered this good life and balance to others. She knew this from occasional conversations with other rooming house or guesthouse proprietors that she ran into at the market or at civic meetings of one sort or another. Madame Maisie never saw these establishments as competition to her own; each offered something special. She never used the term "outsiders" for she didn't consider lodgers or short-term guests to be "outsiders". When they came to the town, guests became, however briefly, part of the community. *Come that ye may partake.*

Madame Maisie never expected to let rooms in her old age. She certainly wasn't raised with such an expectation. But then she didn't suppose it was a profession that anyone really selected, if it could be called a "profession" at all. It was just something one fell into, or back upon, and she was no different. A livelihood, or a way of life. Yes, that was it, a way of life, one that required a generosity of spirit and natural warmth.

Papa wanted her to be a teacher, as her mother was when he met and courted her so many years ago. Maisie was sent to a finishing school so she could learn French, embroidery and fine sewing, elocution, posture, and even some home economics. In fact, Papa thought it important that Maisie attend a finishing school where practical household skills were part of the curriculum, since Bertha, the housekeeper and cook, had her hands full running the house and didn't have time to instruct Maisie. However, Maisie suspected that Papa really didn't want Maisie to spend time in the kitchen with Bertha, although she did anyway.

Bertha never seemed to mind. Well, not exactly. She said she liked the company and she always made sure Maisie didn't get in her way or slow her down. Bertha allowed Maisie to watch but not join in her work. She never explicitly forbade her, but Maisie could tell from the stiffness of Bertha's form and briskness of manner that her own participation was not welcome. Madame Maisie knew that much of what she knew about running a household from cooking fresh brisket and preserving fruit to mopping the floor while maintaining a crisp, professional demeanor was a result of watching Bertha so long ago.

Bertha joined the household shortly after Mama died when Maisie was seven years old. Maisie remembered the quiet that overtook the house after the funeral guests and condolence callers left, not the quiet she worked to maintain for her lodgers, but the quiet of death and perpetuity. There was so much food, overflowing the icebox onto the kitchen and butler's pantry counters. When her mind drifted from reverie, Maisie momentarily thought her parents had hosted a giant party (as her father liked so much to do), but then the dense, seemingly impenetrable quiet jolted her back to reality, to the loss of Mama.

Bertha arrived without much fanfare, without even being introduced to Maisie by Papa and set herself quickly to the task of restoring order in the kitchen. She was dressed in a white uniform. At first, Maisie thought she was a nurse. But as she moved authoritatively around the kitchen, Maisie quickly understood otherwise. Maisie was sure the drink, food, and dirt stains would quickly smudge Bertha's uniform. But they never did. Somehow, Bertha's uniform was as white at the end of the day as at the beginning.

Maisie couldn't even remember exactly when Bertha arrived. Was it just a few days after Mama's death? Longer? In a very short while, Maisie wondered how they had ever managed without Bertha. On the day of her arrival, Maisie watched Bertha intently from the corner of the kitchen as she salvaged what was edible and discarded the rest in the trash bin. In observing Bertha's movements, in her own stasis, she felt that not just the kitchen, but the world itself, was being returned to order.

At some point at the end of this process, as night was beginning to fall, Bertha set some cold cuts and coleslaw on a plate and brought it over to Maisie in the corner. She said, 'My name is Bertha. I know yours since your papa told me,' and then left Maisie to eat her food on a stool in the corner. Bertha finished organizing and cleaning the kitchen just as Maisie finished her supper. Perhaps she even timed it that way. Once she removed Maisie's supper plate and silverware and washed them, the kitchen was in a cleaner, more organized state than it had ever been under Mama's direction.

Despite her strongly held convictions and best intentions regarding home economics and hygiene, Mama was not much of a housekeeper. Maisie never said this to anyone then or hence, but she knew it nevertheless to be the case. Her food was bland at best, and despite Papa's constant badgering her to take on a housekeeper, she never would. Her attentions to detail, never great from the outset, would be even further neglected by her when she drifted into a somnolent daytime state.

Her mother never actually took to her bed as women of a certain class and age did in those days. Instead, she just wafted, from room to room, in the back yard; sometimes, her withdrawal took place when she was stationary, simply sitting on the chair or even the floor. Maisie once asked Papa if Mama had ever been diagnosed with neurasthenia or a similarly vague but at least articulated malady, but he declined to answer.

'Why do you need to know now?' he asked bitterly. When Maisie found herself drifting as a child and young woman, she wondered if she would come to a similarly abrupt yet vague end. She wondered if such an end were, in fact, inevitable for her.

Papa didn't seem surprised (or disappointed) by Mama's passing, Maisie realized in retrospect. Mama's shyness had limited his ambitions quite thoroughly. A banking scion, Papa also had political aspirations on the state and (perhaps someday) the national levels. Mama's charm and gentle beauty seemed to be an asset when they courted. And perhaps they were. But as her charms blurred and her ability to say the right thing at the right time to the right person vanished, Mama declined to host parties. Sometimes, if Papa insisted, Mama disappeared in middle of the party or did not appear at all, leaving him to make excuses on her behalf. Papa stayed away from home for days afterwards, and Maisie was left to forage for herself in the inadequately stocked pantry and larder. For long intervals before Bertha arrived, Maisie ate just enough to survive, until the hunger reached a certain peak, sharpened by a jagged intensity. That's when she knew she'd better find something to tide herself over.

***

Looking out from behind the curtains at the large front window as a potential lodger walked slowly up the flagstone path, Madame Maisie tidied her chignon and removed some lint from her pearl gray cardigan. Madame Maisie judged her to be in her early thirties, although with the hat and the half-veil, it was certainly difficult to tell. She was surprised to see that the lodger had her luggage in tow. Madame Maisie preferred to interview a candidate without luggage. She found an initial luggageless interview to be necessarily easier, more conversational in tone, without the (under)current of desperation that suitcases seemed so often to bring with them. Following the interview, Madame Maisie checked an applicant's references, two at the very least. She accepted references from work supervisors or, to a lesser extent, colleagues as well as residential "overseers" such as landlords. References from friends or family members, however glowing, were assumed to be inflated and therefore not acceptable to Madame Maisie.

She glanced around the room to make sure the parlor and the vestibule were in good order, which they were. The parlor, in particular, was kept dark, so that the damask upholstery of Mama's antique divan wouldn't fade. Madame Maisie knew that she could get it re-upholstered at a discount shop in town, but she wanted to safeguard the same rose-colored fabric that Mama had ordered. Only dignitaries and special guests had been allowed in Mama's front parlor back then. Papa continued that tradition after Mother's passing and insisted that Bertha maintain it to the highest of standards. And to this day, Eunice, a distant relation of Bertha's and her apprentice when she was young, maintained the room and the rooming house as a whole to that same high standard.

Madame Maisie always liked to make a favorable first impression on a potential lodger. Hers was a welcoming house and was known as such in town. When she heard the footsteps pause before the front door, Madame Maisie opened the front door even before the doorbell rang and offered a smile and her extended hand in greeting. She gestured to the young woman to leave her luggage in the vestibule and follow her into the parlor. Merely having the suitcases out of sight often helped the interview proceed more smoothly.

'I'm Maisie. My lodgers call me Madame Maisie. That honorific was given me by Miss Stevens, one of my very first boarders, on account of my having learned French as a young lady. Not that I remember very much of it, now, of course, so don't you try to test me. Yes, I know the words "Madame" and "Maisie" don't seem like a natural pairing, but there you have it. And who might you be, dear?'

'My name is Hannah Leventhal.'

At that pronouncement, Madame Maisie didn't miss a beat. Her smile frozen in place, she reminded herself again that her home was one where all could find welcome.

'I'm surprised you brought luggage to this initial interview, Miss Leventhal. I do believe I've made it clear on all of the circulars around town and in the advertisements in the newspapers that I prefer to meet candidates without luggage. How did you find out about my home?'

'A colleague of mine mentioned it to me.'

Madame Maisie was somewhat taken aback by Miss Leventhal's terse pronouncements. While she didn't consider herself meddlesome, she did like to know more about an applicant before accepting her into what was, after all, her home. Despite its rambling appearance from the exterior, there were only five bedrooms in the home, and one of the rooms was Madame Maisie's. Eunice did not sleep on the premises, as had Bertha before her, preferring instead to ride the streetcar to her home across town. At the time of Miss Leventhal's arrival at the front door, two of the four available bedrooms in the rooming house were empty.

Madame Maisie needed to gain more information about this potential lodger but she also really needed to fill those rooms. That tension continued to play out as she inquired after the young woman's place of employment and references. Here too, Miss Leventhal was brief. She stated that she worked in an old age home and gave her immediate supervisor and a colleague as references.

Madame Maisie understood all too well that rooming houses were shelters for those in transition or those on the outside of conventional familial arrangements. Over the years, all sorts of young ladies had sought and been granted lodgings in her house. There had been actresses, cigarette girls, hostesses, ladies' companions, maids, nurses, office workers, clerks, secretaries, shop girls, showgirls, and waitresses, to name but a few. And it couldn't be known at the outset who would be the most attentive to her and considerate of the other lodgers, the timeliest with the rent check, and the most tidy. Some of the women who seemed the most boisterous would end up being the most quiet and respectful. And vice versa, of course. For all her openness, Madame Maisie was not interested in cultivating a bohemian or even colorful atmosphere. Let the eccentrics go to the other houses! She conducted herself in a manner she believed to be both professional and warm, insisting on combining expectations and instructions as well as stability and comfort. And she expected the same of her lodgers.

This Miss Leventhal made Madame Maisie uneasy in the mind. Certainly, she was tidy in appearance, elegant even in a violet traveling suit and her aforementioned hat with half-veil. But Madame Maisie was struggling to get more than a sentence out of her. She bluntly refused to speak about herself at any length. Or rather, she revealed only the bare minimum. When Madame Maisie stated that she'd like to call her references, Miss Leventhal replied that she was welcome to do so and that she'd wait here in the parlor in the meanwhile. Madame Maisie was not pleased to find that she was being given direction in her own home, that the reins of the interview had somehow been turned over, without warning, to Miss Leventhal.

Her reference was, in fact, glowing. Her supervisor Mr. Van Kirk spoke of an employee of distinction, respected by co-workers, and possessed of skill with the elderly residents, taking care to engage them in conversation and unflinching when it came to dealing with the more unfortunate aspects of aging. For example, if no orderly or bed attendants could be found, Miss Leventhal never hesitated to remove a bedpan or clean up after an accident. She could often be seen guiding a confused resident back to her bedroom if a cane or a walker had been misplaced. Even if she hadn't quite been prepared to hear about bedpans and accidents of nature in a reference call, Madame Maisie appreciated how Mr. Van Kirk spoke of the elderly as residents and not patients or even clients. She felt it added a warm, personal touch, one she herself made every effort to infuse in all of her handlings and doings at the rooming house.

When Madame Maisie returned to the parlor, she found Miss Leventhal exactly where she'd left her. Madame Maisie didn't know where she'd expected her to go, but she did expect her to be standing or with her legs crossed or her gloves removed. In fact, she was in the exact position that Madame Maisie had left her in before making the call. She didn't know what she was going to say until she said it, until she saw Miss Leventhal sitting in that position. She didn't realize she wasn't going to call the second reference, which is what she'd been intending to do, until she saw Miss Leventhal seated with hands folded in lap, not on Mama's damask sofa, but on a wing chair near the front window. Madame Maisie reminded herself to thank Eunice for her excellence in maintaining this room and the home. Sometimes she neglected to express her gratitude. She didn't mean to, but there was always just so much to get done. Even at her most adrift, Mama had never failed to express gratitude.

'You may commence your residence at this house, Miss Leventhal. There are some ground rules. The quiet of all other residents is to be respected at all times. Suppers are eaten communally in the dining room. All other meals are on your own. If you put anything in the icebox, please make sure your name is on it. Guests of any kind male or female are absolutely forbidden in the bedrooms. That is my cardinal rule. Any infringements will result in immediate dismissal without any character reference. This is a respectable house, and I won't have its reputation besmirched in any way. You can stay for as long or as short as you like. All I ask is that you give me one week's notice. Rent is due every Friday by noon. Please follow me to your room.'

Madame Maisie led Miss Leventhal up the staircase, with its grapes-and-vines stained glass window above the love seat on the landing, and to the bedroom at the end of the corridor. All of the rooms in Madame Maisie's rooming house were furnished tastefully, with furniture selected by Mama and purchased by Papa still in outstanding working order. Madame Maisie kept the rooms feminine and subdued in shades such as burgundy, gray, lavender, plum, and wine. Besides the twin bed, each room had a night table, a comfortable reading chair, and a writing desk. And there was plenty of lighting, as well. In addition to the natural light from the large window, the room featured an overhead light fixture, a lamp on the night table, and a desk lamp. Madame Maisie informed Miss Leventhal that there were two washrooms in the corridor, one at each end. Papa had been pleased with that abundance and whenever he mentioned it to guests, Mama blushed in mortification. At such moments, it was all too evident to Maisie that Mama thought that Papa's bluster and braggadocio were more detrimental to Papa's career than her spells and fragility of spirit.

Madame Maisie left Miss Leventhal in her new accomodations. A quick glance around the room and a nod of the head indicated Miss Leventhal's approval. Instead of checking in with Eunice, as she usually liked to do at this time, Madame Maisie retreated to her own bedroom, or rather, the solarium adjoining it. This room was composed almost entirely of panels of glass and filled with spectacular light at all times of day. Plants and flowers of many varieties ferns, orchids, Christmas cactus, philodendron, spider plants, snake plants thrived here. Bertha and then Eunice were equally gifted with green thumbs.

When Mama was alive, she insisted on tending the greenery. She moved among them carefully and slowly, removing dead leaves. On one particularly drizzly day, Maisie entered the room, wanting to surprise Mama with her perfect spelling exam, and glimpsed her among the plants and trees, a spectral presence seemingly floating above them into the mist itself. She left the room without sharing with Mama the results of the spelling exam.

Today, however, Madame Maisie needed to recover from the interview with Miss Leventhal. She bent down and reached for the handle of the wicker chair to steady herself before lowering her body into its ample cushions. She hoped she hadn't been too severe when laying down the rule about guests in the bedroom. But she couldn't be strict enough on that front. She couldn't afford another incident along the lines of the one that occurred some ten years ago with a Miss Simpson. That lodger had brought in a female guest, and had been heard by other guests making all sorts of sounds clearly of an unspeakable nature. And yet spoken they were. Another lodger mentioned to Madame Maisie kissing, laughter, moaning, and worse of all, a steady squeaking of bedsprings. Madame Maisie did not wish to dwell on what took place in that room; she hated to even hear those conveying such unseemly behavior spoken in her home. She felt as if the home, the very air its residents breathed, had been soiled. And she knew she had to take action immediately to avoid the permanent besmirching of her home's (now near) spotless reputation.

When she confronted Miss Simpson with the charges that had brought to her attention, Miss Simpson not only didn't deny them but actually affirmed them. She cited Madame Maisie's house rule (at the time) about no male guests and insisted that she had done nothing wrong. Madame Maisie told Miss Simpson in no certain terms that she had to pack her things and leave at once. Miss Simpson probably could have hired a lawyer to fight the eviction but fortunately she had not done so. Madame Maisie would have hated to see her rooming house dragged through the legal system. Miss Simpson departed the rooming house that very evening. Immediately after her departure, Madame Maisie herself scrubbed the floors, furniture surfaces, and even the walls. She removed the bed lines, blankets, and pillows and burned them all in the backyard. As a result of this episode, Madame Maisie amended the house rules from no male guests in bedrooms to no guests in bedrooms at all. And she had maintained that policy ever since. Madame Maisie took pride in the compliments regularly paid her by the neighbors on the respectability of her rooming house. They, like Madame Maisie, knew all too well that a home of ill repute could have blighted, and perhaps even destroyed, the block and the neighborhood.

Madame Maisie told herself there was no cause to regret her impulsiveness or misgivings in general regarding Miss Leventhal. She was a respectable young woman with suitable employment and an outstanding character reference. She would do well here, surely. And the rooming house would benefit from her presence. All the lodgers contributed something of themselves to the spirit of her house. Still, the uneasiness lingered, even here in the solarium. When she heard Eunice's tread in the corridor outside, she rose to discuss with her the meal plan for the evening and the day ahead.

***

As the weeks and months passed, Madame Maisie's unease did indeed appear unwarranted. Miss Leventhal got along well with both of the other young ladies in residence Miss Stella Norcliffe, an actress, and Miss Agnes Robertson, a typist at an insurance firm. Miss Norcliffe was in town for a drawing room comedy whose run had been extended several times. She had a prominent role, as the confidante of the leading lady, and much of the play's momentum depended on her comic timing and delivery. Miss Robertson tried to pump her for information about the theater and its stars but Miss Norcliffe was always quite reticent to share. She claimed she didn't really know them very well outside of rehearsals and performances and that acting was a profession like any other, only with poorly heated dressing rooms and an uncertain salary.

Madame Maisie once went to see Miss Norcliffe in her onstage role and was stunned at the transformation. The demure resident of her rooming house had been transformed into a madcap tour-de-force, with exaggerated wide eyes, squeaky voice, batting eyelids, and spouting dialogue laced with double entendre. Even her curls, which seemed golden in the glow of the dining room chandelier of the rooming house, took on brassy tones under the lights of the theater. The audience loved her. Madame Maisie was amused, despite her better judgment and refined sensibility, and proud too to see one of her girls make good.

Miss Leventhal never joined in Miss Robertson's questioning nor did she follow up on any of Miss Norcliffe's responses. But Madame Maisie saw her dark eyes take in all that was going on around her. And she noticed that Miss Leventhal was unfailingly polite to everyone, particularly Eunice. She always took great care to thank Eunice for her service and compliment her on the delicious meals.

With her natural warmth and charm, Miss Robertson did attempt to draw out Miss Leventhal. But she was unable to elicit much of a response. Madame Maisie was secretly relieved to discover that Miss Leventhal didn't behave in this terse manner only to her. If Miss Robertson couldn't get more out of her, how could she, Madame Maisie, be expected to? Madame Maisie was particularly fond of Miss Robertson and her conversational grace and acumen. She imagined Mama was similarly gifted before her decline.

Although Madame Maisie took care not to inquire about the pasts of the residents, some volunteered information, or it just slipped out, or something in between. Sometimes they lingered in the dining room, spirits high and guard low after Eunice's feasts. For example, Miss Norcliffe confessed that her parents were not pleased with her choice of the stage as a profession. Miss Robertson disclosed that her elderly parents were glad she'd found work in an office but wanted to see her "settled down" very soon. At thirty-eight, Miss Robertson showed no signs of doing any such thing, although Madame Maisie liked to think of her rooming house as a "settling down" of sorts. Miss Robertson was Madame Maisie's only lodger whom she was tempted to ask if she could address her by her Christian name. Only she never did. The dictates of decorum were too strong; she absolutely could not overstep the boundaries that she herself had established, that her rooming house required.

Madame Maisie was sometimes tempted to reveal more about her own past, but always restrained herself. After her schooling concluded and after her coming out, Maisie did not lack for suitors, some of them quite eligible. One of them, James van Eggle, had been particularly handsome and persistent. Maisie was flattered by the attention and excitement, of course, but she never could quite visualize herself in the role of a wife and a mother. The finality of those roles, the tether to a man and a child presented such a stark contrast to the playful socializing of courting, at which she excelled. And then there was always the house to run (with Bertha) and civic improvement committees to lead and, of course, Papa required tending. Even as he relinquished the idea of a career in politics, he expected Maisie to serve as hostess, which she charmingly, unfailingly did, drawing upon her powers of flirtation and general ability to keep conversation flowing smoothly and social events proceeding apace. When Papa died years later, it was too late to think of marriage (or so it seemed to Maisie) and so she had to turn to letting rooms. None of this seemed very suitable for post-dinner conversation, even of the stays-loosened sort, and so Maisie never shared any of it. Besides, the lady of the house was expected to exercise greater self-control in any situation.

Of course, Miss Leventhal never lingered after dinner or any other time, for that matter. As soon as dinner concluded, she bade all a good night and climbed the stairs to her room. None of the others commented on her departure, on her holding herself apart. The conversation continued, with Madame Maisie making sure it never veered too far off course or color.

One night, as Madame Maisie was sitting in the solarium illuminated solely by candlelight, she heard footsteps pass quietly by. At this point, she could recognize Miss Leventhal's tread. Madame Maisie knew the steps of all the lodgers. She knew all of the sounds of the home, which windows rattled when northern winds came and groaned when opened in the spring and summer, which floorboards creaked the most, the length of the icebox's song, the shuddering of the very walls themselves unexpectedly when there appeared to be no stimulus for such inward movement. If others speculated about the haunting of the house, Madame Maisie just laughed. This was her home, as it had been Mama's and Papa's, and here she lived with her young women. She knew its every movement, and if there were ghosts or spirits, she was quite sure she would be the first to know.

Madame Maisie was surprised to discover that Miss Leventhal's footsteps now began regularly to pass by her room. Not always at the same time but still nearly every night. Miss Leventhal had never demonstrated such activity in the nearly six months of her residence, and Madame Maisie was taken aback. Of course, there was no curfew per se in the rooming house regulations, but such late night movement was most untoward. Madame Maisie did not wish to question Miss Leventhal on the nature of her movements. Miss Leventhal was a grown woman with freedom of movement. Nor did she wish to change the house's regulations. Such a change could alter the equilibrium, so carefully cultivated, of the house.

One night, instead of changing into her nightwear, Madame Maisie waited in the solarium in her evening dress, a gray, high-collared one, to be precise. After Miss Leventhal passed her room and after she heard the front door close, Madame Maisie descended the stairs and exited just as quietly out the door.

Fortunately, the light from the moon and the streetlamps enabled Madame Maisie to follow Miss Leventhal with a relative degree of ease. Despite her advanced years, Madame Maisie was able to keep pace. Her curiosity and determination would not allow her to flag. And she was pleased that she'd remembered to wear her walking shoes, with their comfort and lightness so that Ms. Leventhal would not hear her footsteps behind her. She followed Miss Leventhal through her own neighborhood, largely well-maintained, despite an abandoned home here and there, to a neighborhood quite decrepit and growing increasingly so the further (and further) she walked. Although it wasn't very far away, Madame Maisie had never been here. There were no railroad tracks as a dividing line; it wasn't literally the proverbial "wrong side of the tracks". It simply wasn't a suitable destination for respectable folk. There were boarded up houses, crooked houses, shacks really, all crowded very closely to the street. There were very few streetlamps now, and besides an occasional dog barking or trash drifting by the window, very little sound, either. Madame Maisie saw Miss Leventhal knock on a door of the one of the shacks and then enter. Whether she had been granted entrance or entered of her own accord Madame Maisie couldn't be certain.

Through the window, Madame Maisie saw Miss Leventhal take a baby girl, with coloring and hair nearly identical to Miss Leventhal's own swarthy skin and dark and curly, nearly kinky, hair into her outstretched arms and transformed countenance. That was the only way Madame Maisie could describe it transformed. Instead of the ramrod bearing and blank facial expression, here was lightness of face and body and gesture. Miss Leventhal swung the baby through the air, as she giggled and gurgled in a delight equal to that of the woman who held and played with her. Concealed in the shadows, Madame Maisie couldn't be sure how long she stared at the pair. She realized she'd need to get back now since she wouldn't have the retreating back of Miss Leventhal as her guide on the return trip.

Somehow Madame Maisie made it back to the rooming house with speed and without incident. She shut the front door just as quietly on the return trip and ascended to her bedroom and the solarium. Instead of lighting a lamp or even a candle, Madame Maisie sat in the darkness, or rather the light of the moon. Sleep was out of the question, of course. She wished there was someone she could turn to at that moment. Mama wouldn't have known what to do; Papa would have been indifferent to the situation, to "women's problems". Eunice had family matters of her own. Madame Maisie never knew what those were since Eunice never shared and only responded, 'Fine' or 'It was good' when Madame Maisie inquired about her day off. Bertha, who cared for Maisie following the passing of Mama, would have known. Maisie never considered Bertha to be her "second mother". She wasn't that naïve or sentimental; neither was Bertha. But she knew Bertha would have risen to this occasion. Madame Maisie felt Bertha's absence more strongly that night than she ever had before since Bertha's passing. How many years ago was that?

But Madame Maisie had to handle this situation by herself, without the guidance of Bertha, without any guidance at all. Now, for the first time in her long life, Madame Maisie found herself utterly unmoored. She'd worked so hard to build a reputable establishment, one that served as a beacon for wayfarers of all kinds. This was a place where hard-working women could find lodgings and rest, as they made their way in the world without the (visible) aid or involvement of men. In this house bequeathed to her by her parents, she had made a way for herself.

There was something in the example of Miss Leventhal that compelled her. Beneath her blankness, there was a steely resolve, one that took her to a rooming house with luggage to the initial interview, one that brought her to a dining room with civility but with minimal engagement, one that took her into unsavory neighborhoods to follow and foster a primordial bond. And yet Madame Maisie's boarding house depended on her reputation and that of its lodgers. If those reputations flagged, her livelihood would collapse, and so would the house itself, with its carefully preserved interiors and exterior.

Even if no explicit house rule had been broken, Madame Maisie felt that her moral code had been breached, her trust violated. She felt herself exposed to a raw indecorousness, as she had never been with her mother's descent and her father's wandering eye, despite the rumors about him that always got back to her and despite what she saw at house parties within these very walls and even during church services, over the years. Although she had lived her entire life in the walls of this house, Madame Maisie did not consider herself sheltered. She knew well enough of life's cruelties, but surely there were limits even to her benevolence. How dare Miss Leventhal bring her own disgrace to the threshold of Madame Maisie's rooming house! And how foolish, how reckless of Madame Maisie to allow said disgrace to cross her threshold!

Madame Maisie again reminded herself that sleep would not come to her tonight. She who always welcomed sleep, even during the nights after her mother's passing, even during the daytime throughout the years, just like her mother, would not encounter it in the hours ahead. Madame Maisie did not pace the floors nor did she invoke the visages or the wisdom of the three who had loved her. For the remainder of the night, she would not harken back to the time before the word "Madame" had been added to her name, before she had become a host mother to strangers. Strangers? Yes, alas in the end, after everything strangers. *Ach* … Madame Maisie sat unmoving on the wicker chair, anchored (as much as was possible) in the here and now, perhaps as Miss Leventhal had sat on her first day in this house, until a decision came to her, until the sun rose and conveyed light into this chamber constructed in its honor, until the sounds of the first streetcar of the day could be heard outside.

"Lettering and the Art of Living"

Sylvia donned her tortoiseshell reading glasses and placed the envelope on the kitchen table covered by a white cloth with a strawberry border. She'd only laid the tablecloth down last night and was pleased it had very few stains, although she'd had it for a very long time. It had been bequeathed to her by her mother, may she rest in peace.

The envelope looked significant enough to be opened with the letter-opener Sylvia received from her friend Bernice. A letter-opener was different from a paper knife, Bernice declared when presenting the gift years ago on the occasion of Sylvia's birthday, shortly after they first met. Bernice ought to have known since her father was a stationer by profession and taught Bernice all there was to know about fine paper. This letter-opener had a cedar handle carved with a grapes and vines pattern. Sylvia wondered if it came from the Holy Land, but she never asked Bernice. If Bernice told her, that would have been different.

Ordinary daily mail was not opened with the letter-opener given to Sylvia by Bernice. Envelopes containing bills, promotional flyers, and sweepstakes won (or assured to have been won if just one more form were completed) were simply torn open. Only special handwritten letters from family or friends were carefully opened with the letter-opener gifted by Bernice. If someone took the time to write Sylvia by hand, then she would take the time to open the envelope properly. That was just something Sylvia believed strongly in.

Over the years, Sylvia had mostly received letters from her mother. The letters were filled with the news from back home: the births, graduations, bar mitzvahs, and deaths, of course. But sometimes her mother sent her a new casserole or lasagna recipe she'd tried out with the "girls" in her mah-jong club, or some new lemon squares. Sylvia loved the juxtaposition of the tartness of the lemon with the sweetness of the powdered sugar that covered the lemon squares. Or even a fresh salad with walnuts or sunflower seeds, if one of the girls were dieting, which was quite often the case.

Her mother first wrote to Sylvia after she'd left home for secretarial school. Although Sylvia quickly mastered touch-typing, her mother always insisted that she write to her by hand. 'Always work on your penmanship,' her mother instilled in Sylvia from an early age and repeated over and over. Her mother's own handwriting, with its long yet rounded lettering, was a source of pride. Sylvia knew early on that her handwriting couldn't approach her mother's in overall elegance and would never win prizes the way her mother's had, but it was still a clear, legible hand. Nothing to be ashamed of, that's for sure, and Sylvia never was.

The envelope in today's mail, written in a spiky script, was addressed to Miss Sylvia Hirschfein. She felt a start of surprise since it had been quite a while since she'd received a handwritten piece of mail. She could tell at once that it was a letter and not a card by the weight of the envelope. Sylvia still occasionally received New Year's and season's greeting cards from the children and grandchildren of co-workers from the front office of the ladies hosiery firm where she worked for decades as a secretary. Of course, her co-workers themselves had long since passed away.

Suddenly, Sylvia thought longingly of Mavis, with whom she shared lunch once a week for years at a cafeteria near work. House salad and a coffee black no sugar. That was Mavis' order every week. She loved how Mavis never glanced at the menu or hesitated before ordering. And she always did say those words, even if the waitress surely knew what her order would be. Mavis never had much to say during their lunches – little office gossip, less news from home – but Sylvia always enjoyed her company. Poor Mavis, gone so young, breast cancer. Sylvia stayed with Mavis in the hospice until the terrible end, her moans and cries embedded in Sylvia's skin and mind. If there were friends or relatives, they were never there when Sylvia was.

Of course, now her co-workers' children had grown children of their own. And none of them used the written-out "Miss" address. It was always "Sylvia Hirschfein" or "Ms. Sylvia Hirschfein", or occasionally, the erroneous "Mrs. Sylvia Hirschfein". Sylvia took pride in her work as a secretary – in her speedy, error-free typing, her note taking, her ability to keep the office running smoothly, her overall professionalism. When, towards the end of her career, her boss offered to change her title to "administrative assistant", Sylvia insisted on remaining a "secretary". That was what she had been and would continue to be. In her retirement, she told people she was a secretary by profession.

Sylvia relished receiving greeting cards and unfailingly responded with a card of her own. She never purchased cards in packets; she just didn't want to send the same card to different people. Even if the sentiment were the same and even if she knew the recipients wouldn't communicate with each other about which card she'd sent to them, Sylvia wanted each card to be different. But then the stationery store a few blocks over closed down. And then Sylvia's arthritis and varicose veins made it hard for her to take the bus to the next neighborhood to buy other cards. And then a few years later, the post office closed. And so Sylvia couldn't even get stamps to write a note on lined paper from the school notebooks she'd saved. "Consolidation" was the word used at the time of the post office's closing. Even more than her own physical decline, Sylvia felt her world narrowed, irrevocably diminished, by the closing of the stationery store and the post office.

Given the longevity of her card exchange tradition, Sylvia felt terrible not being able to return the cards. She tried to find the numbers of the card senders in the telephone books so she could at least call them, but the numbers were unlisted. Sylvia had heard about the computers and the Internet, of course, but she didn't know how to get started with all of that. She just hoped the card senders, the children of her co-workers in the front office of the ladies hosiery firm, could somehow sense her good wishes. Perhaps not very likely in most cases, but still Sylvia hoped.

In the fine cut of the paper of the envelope now before her, Sylvia could see Bernice's tacit approval. Bernice always insisted one had to feel the paper itself with one's own (ungloved) hands before buying it. They met in the stationery store a block from the secretarial school where both were enrolled only three months after their courses began. She and Bernice laughed that they met off-campus instead of in class or in the cafeteria even. Bernice's first words to Sylvia at the stationery store were: 'Not a good choice. That paper's going to turn brown and crumble in no time.'

Sylvia whirled around to meet the speaker of those words. And there was Bernice, smiling broadly, lips a bright strawberry, brown hair perfectly bobbed, and wearing a fitted forest green dress suit. Sylvia smiled in return; she couldn't help herself. Bernice immediately linked her arm in Sylvia's and led her to the paper stock that she thought Sylvia should purchase. It was creamy and thick enough so you couldn't see through it even when it was held up to the light. Bernice demonstrated for Sylvia so she could see for herself.

After they left the stationery store, Bernice invited Sylvia for a milk shake at the soda fountain down the street. Bernice explained that sometimes you just had to splurge a little; it was good for the soul. Sylvia just took all of this in, hardly knowing what to say. Sitting in the drugstore booth, staring at the vanilla froth around the strawberry painted lips moving ever so rapidly, Sylvia felt out of breath. Breathless with Bernice.

In turning the letter over, Sylvia saw that there was no return address. Bernice contended that there were always several possibilities when it came to letters without return addresses. The sender could be lazy, a liar/scam artist, a secret admirer, or "simply" aiming for an air of mystery. Senders of the first sort could usually be ruled out by the quality of the envelope and penmanship; a lazy person just wouldn't go to all that trouble to create a good first impression. Senders of the last three sorts always had to be looked out for, though. Liar/scam artists had to be avoided. Admiration of the secret sort never did anyone any good, really. Bernice liked to be admired openly, freely. And while a sense of mystery could heighten the pleasure, it could also create a false sense of expectation. Bernice always preferred to include her return address on the flap of the envelope, of course, and not in the top left hand corner of the envelope front.

And Bernice certainly did know a great deal about admiration openly offered. After they agreed to share an apartment (since it would be both prudent and fun) after graduation, Sylvia discovered the extent of the admiration of Bernice. If she'd thought beforehand, she could warrant a larger, or at least more focused, share of Bernice's attention as her roommate, Sylvia discovered she was mistaken. It wasn't long before the dimensions of the admiration's extent, the very breadth and intensity of the sunlight that was Bernice, became clear. Bouquets of the most extravagant kind were always in abundance in their apartment. Roses of every shape and hue in the living room; in the dining room, calla lilies, carnations, hydrangeas, and others. Once, a bouquet of fuchsia orchids on the vestibule table stopped Sylvia in her tracks when she first came home. Although her own name was so much more romantic than Bernice's, it was Bernice who had commandeered all the romance in the household, seemingly in the whole town. This irony was never lost on Sylvia, and it hit her especially hard during that initial sighting of the fuchsia orchids on the vestibule table.

Boxes of chocolates arrived too truffles, pralines, nougats, and bon bons of every sort but Bernice never ate them. She said they were terrible for her figure, but she never discouraged the admirers from giving them to her. For that matter, they didn't do wonders for Sylvia's figure, which while it had never been the hourglass one of Bernice, had at least been sturdy and trim. But with the chocolates, that figure began to slacken perceptibly. Sylvia had come across the word "blowsy" once and knew she had to be careful or she could quickly land in the realm of that word. Still, she couldn't help herself. She couldn't refrain from Bernice's romantic discards. They couldn't really be called "leftovers", since Bernice never opened the boxes of chocolates at all. Sylvia saw the indignity of her consumption of Bernice's chocolates, and still she couldn't help herself. Even when she was nauseous with their sweetness, even when she felt as if the insides of her belly were smeared with chocolate and her soul sprinkled with pralines. Better Bernice's discards than nothing at all. Besides, if Sylvia didn't eat them, Bernice would have thrown them out. Or so Bernice insisted.

To Sylvia, worse than the chocolates were the stories Bernice regaled her with on the evenings following her dates. There was the man who worked for a different company but in the same office building, a copy editor of some sort. And the one with whom she was set up by a co-worker of hers, a vacuum cleaner salesman. And the music teacher who really doted on her and always came to the front door and insisted on saying, 'Good evening' to Sylvia. Bernice didn't share very many stories about the music teacher the next day. And there were so many others, of course. None of them came into sharp focus now (or possibly even then) for Sylvia. But she always listened to the stories, never begged off.

Bernice basked in the adoration of men, however fleeting it always turned out be. There was always a mother who was not pleased, parents who thought their son could "do better", a returning girlfriend who seemed to be more stable, more suitable "wife material", as something was off, or not quite right. Even the music teacher, with his solicitous gaze and impeccable manners, pulled away, although sometimes Sylvia wondered if it had been Bernice, in fact, who had tired of him.

Fingering again the paper of the envelope before her, Sylvia heard noises in the apartment above hers. There were obscenities shouted, a thud to the floor, then whimpering and sobbing. None of this was unusual anymore. Sylvia didn't know what to do. She had never become accustomed to it exactly, but her options were limited, non-existent, really. Once she knocked on that apartment door. The burly man glared down at her for a minute and slammed the door in her face. The police wouldn't come for a domestic dispute, if it could even be called that. Since they occurred so regularly, arguments and physical confrontation were more like their modus operandi, their preferred means of communication. In fact, the police hardly ever came into this neighborhood at all. The building and this neighborhood had descended so low over the years; she wondered if they would ever come back. If she would still be alive, if ever they did come back.

There was one man, one of Bernice's admirers, who was especially unworthy of her. Charlie. Sylvia remembered his name, of course. Bernice was with him, longer than the others, although just how long Sylvia would never know, as it turned out. Charlie never came to the door, and Bernice never introduced him to Sylvia. He wasn't that good-looking, from what Sylvia could tell. She could see that his mouth was always set in a scowl, that his suits, even if of fine cut, were always rumpled and could barely contain his body, which wasn't exactly muscular or fat, but kind of both. He was strong, that's for sure. Sylvia wasn't eager to get on his bad side. She could see all of that from behind the lace curtains at the front window her mother had sewn for her after she had given her mother the windows' dimensions just before the young graduates had first moved into the apartment.

Sylvia removed her reading glasses from her nose and left them to rest on their chain against her chest. She walked away from the envelope to the window to look out on the courtyard below. The superintendent had once taken great care to maintain it. There used to be flowerbeds and an outdoor glider around the pruned oak tree in the center. The flowerbeds and the glider were gone now. Trash junk food bags and wrappers, promotional brochures, and the like drifted through the yard. Only the tree remained, still sturdy despite not having been pruned in years. Sylvia liked to gaze upon it, gaining inspiration from its perseverance and marking the seasons' change by the colors of its leaves.

When Bernice came home that night Sylvia still thought of it as "that night" the weather had been rather like today's, with a similar crispness of air. Sylvia was reading in her room, having eaten a light barley soup for dinner. She heard Bernice enter the apartment slowly, fumblingly. This was quite unlike Bernice's characteristically brisk entrance: a quick close of the door, a pouring of the keys into the bowl on the vestibule table once graced by the fuchsia orchids.

When Sylvia emerged from her bedroom into the corridor, she gasped in shock. Bernice's left eye was black and blue and many other shades; her face was all swollen. Sylvia accompanied her to the bathroom and helped minister first-aid as best she could. There really wasn't much in the medicine cabinet that would help here some iodine, some aloe. Sylvia brought some raw meat from the fridge and some ice from the freezer. She sat on the floor, while Bernice sat on the toilet seat with its lid down.

Even having spied on Charlie from behind the living room curtains all these times, Bernice was still taken aback by the extent of the beating. Her Bernice, her beautiful Bernice, with the wide smile framed by strawberry-colored lips and the bobbed curls. Sylvia was overcome, not by the sense of the world's injustice for she had long ago accommodated herself to, if not accepted, that injustice. Sometimes, she felt that it was etched into the pores of her skin, into every fiber of her being. Rather, she was overcome by a longing to do more, to be able to protect Bernice. This sense of impotence caused her to do something she'd never done, something in retrospect, of course, she never should have done. She leaned into Bernice's stockinged calves, put her arms around them, and declared:

'Bernice, you have to leave Charlie.'

Bernice stood up, meat and ice cubes against her face, and walked out of the bathroom and Sylvia's (waking) life forever. Remaining on the bathroom floor, Sylvia heard Bernice packing all of her suitcases, without deliberation or care. Eventually, she arose from the bathroom floor, returned to her bedroom, and fell into sleep. She thought she heard the front door close at some point, but couldn't be sure, didn't want to know. The next morning, Sylvia found the check for this and next month's rent paid in full. Even in her abandonment, Bernice's generosity moved Sylvia.

The envelope called Sylvia back to the present day, but she wasn't quite ready to open it. She remembered that she didn't only receive cards from the children of her co-workers. Sylvia also received invitations to the bar mitzvahs and weddings of the children of her distant cousin Rochelle, whose name had been changed to Rahel when her family became ultra-Orthodox. Some of the envelopes were addressed by hand, but lately they were in a fancy pseudo-calligraphy executed by a computer made to look handwritten. This was a subtlety Bernice taught Sylvia all those years ago, although back then the practice of mechanized writing on the envelope was far less common than today. Bernice once said that the term "lettering" was needed to describe all aspects of the letter: the letters of the words, the quality of the paper of the letter, the style of the letter, and the envelope, including what was written on it. All of that could not be encompassed in the term "letter-writing".

The invitations on card stock that came from Rahel were mailed from Israel. They were usually cream-colored, sometimes egg shell or pale gray or taupe. The first letters of the bar mitzvah boy's name would be shaped into a set of *tefilin* on the front of the invitation. The letters of the bride and groom would be similarly woven into an artful design. Sylvia hadn't advanced very far with her Hebrew studies, but she could still decipher the letters. Her mother, raising her alone and with no financial assistance, insisted on that. She took Sylvia to the nearby synagogue which had a Sunday school and somehow managed to get her enrolled. Sylvia watched this take place while standing in the hallway of the synagogue's school and furtively looking through the door of the classroom window. Her mother just wouldn't take no for an answer, as they say.

After her marriage, Rahel and her husband migrated to Israel. Ever since she received that letter opener from Bernice (which may or may not have come from Israel), Sylvia always wanted to travel there. Israel was a vision that shimmered before her – a land of oranges, sun, and ravishing women in army fatigues but nevertheless a place palpable, a cosmic space larger than her mother and herself and her secretarial job at the ladies' hosiery firm. Whenever she visited her mother, Sylvia put away money in the pale blue box for the Jewish National Fund that her mother kept near the toaster. But if she wondered if she'd live to see the building and the neighborhood "come up", Sylvia also knew she'd never now reach the land of Israel.

Before Rahel and her husband migrated, long before Sylvia received those invitations, she and her mother attended Rahel and her husband's wedding. It was a lovely affair, with the men and women seated separately. Sylvia enjoyed watching the women dance – the fellowship and grace of it without masculine intervention – even if neither she nor her mother participated. Both were dressed modestly, in charcoal and black dresses respectively, but Sylvia didn't know the dance steps, which, though they appeared to be simple, were, in fact, quite elaborate. She knew she would've been allowed into the dance circle, but she didn't want to attract any undue attention by her ignorance. Sylvia also felt especially ungainly in a dress, which she hadn't worn in years. And even if she could've mastered the steps, Sylvia didn't want to leave her mother at the table without a conversation partner. The fact that they weren't Orthodox would be apparent to all attendees by telltale signs: skin visible at the neck, her mother's white, unwigged hair, something intangible that set them both apart. Yet if no one besides Rahel (who was busy being the bride!) spoke to them, no one seemed to mind their attendance, either.

Sylvia returned from her reverie and decided it was time to cut the envelope with the letter opener from Bernice. She cut it carefully, slowly, aware that her hands were trembling more than they usually did. Funny how her mother never took to Bernice, felt that she wasn't a good influence on her Sylvia. The one time they'd met had not gone well. Bernice's charm had fallen very flat and fizzled away. Her mother quickly gathered her things and left for the bus station. Her mother's assessment of her friend which came to Sylvia in her letter the following weekend was unnecessary. Both Sylvia and Bernice knew how she felt. Sylvia was tempted to show her mother's letter to Bernice. She thought Bernice might chuckle; she wanted to hear Bernice's particularly throaty chuckle when she was at once amused and slightly displeased. But Sylvia never did show Bernice that letter.

When she removed the letter from the envelope, at first the words didn't make sense. She checked to make sure that her reading glasses were on, even though, of course, Sylvia had seen the words. There were words and phrases such as

43

"redevelopment" and "repurposing" and "mixed use" and, more ominously, "vacating the premises" and "failure to comply". It took Sylvia a moment to realize that the "premises" under discussion in this letter were this home, her efficiency apartment. She'd lived here for decades, since shortly after Bernice left her for destinations unknown. Sylvia never did find out where and never tried to track her down. When she thought "left her", Sylvia had to catch herself. Bernice had never really been "with her", truth be told. No matter how deeply Sylvia had yearned for that to be the case. Her beautiful Bernice, *la bella Bernice*. After Bernice was gone, Sylvia used to play with alliteration before drifting into sleep.

Sylvia put her hands on the table, clasped around the letter, noting how swollen and flecked with brown spots her hands were. If Bernice were still alive, she wouldn't have let her hands reach such a state, Sylvia thought. It was too early to go to bed. Instead she decided to sit in the one easy chair in the apartment, the one opposite the kitchen table. Next to it was a side table, on which her mother's portrait stood. Taken just before her passing, her mother peered from the frame, as steely and unflinching as ever. When Bernice left, Sylvia never told her mother. She didn't see the point, but she wondered if her mother sensed it anyway. Mothers always know. In those months after Bernice's departure, Sylvia thought about her father, not for the first time certainly, but intensively, relentlessly, as if the grief over both the loss of Bernice and never knowing her father had become intertwined, undistinguishable even.

After staring at her mother's portrait, Sylvia's eyes roamed the walls of her efficiency apartment. Or was it a studio? Sylvia never really knew the difference between the two. In any case, "efficiency" was more applicable. Sylvia was nothing if not efficient and never struggled with her small space. Her home was more than enough for her. Unlike her colleagues who bemoaned their inadequate urban living quarters bursting with tchotchkes and memorabilia, Sylvia collected nothing. Aside from the few work clothes she'd once needed and the furniture basics, there was very little in her apartment.

Even her refrigerator was only lightly stocked. After she threw away the remaining chocolates when Bernice left her, Sylvia stopped eating sweets altogether. She now kept her figure trim on salads delivered by the one grocery store willing to drive into the neighborhood. And if her figure was less sturdy with advancing age, it nonetheless remained trim. Surveying her home from the one armchair, Sylvia wondered who could possibly want this efficiency apartment and with such urgency, such vehemence. And how absurd, how cruel, to have addressed the envelope by hand. "Failure to comply" indeed!

Of course, Sylvia knew the whole building, even the whole block, would soon be torn down. She wasn't surprised by this; it was probably a good thing for the city, she had to admit. There were big plans for the area, with its proximity to the water and the city. Rahel had commented on that proximity when she came to visit Sylvia after her mother passed away, quietly in her sleep. Rahel said it must be nice to live in such a convenient, central location. Sylvia only smiled in agreement, helping Rahel take off her coat and hanging it neatly in the one closet. Rahel insisted on coming, even though Sylvia wasn't really up to it and just wanted to lie in bed. But she couldn't refuse Rahel; she couldn't deprive her mother of the honor of her single condolence caller. There were no mirrors to cover in Sylvia's apartment, except the one on the small medicine cabinet door, since Sylvia hated to look at herself in the mirror even on the best of days.

Rahel and Sylvia sat together largely in silence, since Sylvia wasn't sure what was acceptable to convey to Rahel about her mother who never married, who raised a daughter alone, and who never tried to fix Sylvia up with men she knew were "looking". Somehow, she felt Rahel understood without Sylvia's saying anything at all. During that condolence call, Sylvia was tempted to ask Rahel if she'd ever heard anything about her father, but she never did. It was her mother's day, after all.

Night was closing in on her. And on the building and neighborhood, too, Sylvia thought with a smile. Sylvia stood up from the armchair, returned the letter to the envelope, and then placed the envelope in a walnut box in her bureau drawer with the letter opener alongside. She didn't really know where she'd go at this late date, with her arthritis and varicose veins and swollen, brown-speckled hands. The assisted living facilities that she'd seen advertised on television, with their glossy, beige interiors and residents rolling along merrily in their motorized wheelchairs, were all, of course, out of reach for her. Who would have her?

But Sylvia knew she'd find a way. Just as she'd found a way after Bernice left her, just as she'd found a way after her mother had passed away. Her mother, who raised Sylvia by herself, to be equally self-reliant, to know the Hebrew alphabet, would have had it no other way, would not have allowed her to give in. Sylvia could hear her mother now, as the refrigerator began its song. She could her mother's voice as she donned her coat after a visit to this very apartment in a building soon to be razed, imploring Sylvia to remember to write. And not rote one-pagers, either, but letters, as they were meant to be written, with reflection and insight. And in tidy, unhurried penmanship, of course, so that she could show them off to her neighbors, so that she could know that her child, her one-and-only, was well in the world.

"Undressing After Sinai"

When Sore descended from the bus, she was curious to see how the avenue had changed. She wondered if it would be different from the avenue she'd walked only six months before. It was the central artery of the neighborhood she'd known all of her life, or at least one she'd thought she'd known. The shops appeared to be the same. Sore could see that at a quick glance.

The butcher shop, with its many meat options on display, was open, and the same butcher in the bloodstained apron stood behind the counter. Yes, he was the one who used to wink at Sore and always insisted on serving her himself when she was running errands for her mother. Although she never questioned her obligation to shoulder the bulk of the errands as the eldest daughter, this was one that Sore never enjoyed, dreaded even. Maybe it was because of the raw meat, a living creature extinguished, slashed into choice cut, or slab. No, it wasn't that. She was no vegetarian. The butcher's leer and his refusal to speak beyond the bare minimum needed for the business transaction, along with the blood on his apron, seemed only to heighten his lust and Sore's revulsion. As he handed over the meat packages, Sore felt that she was drowning in blood, in the lascivious embrace of death itself. Sore didn't linger today before the window display.

The same grocery store was there. She almost added "of course" in her mind, but caught herself. Sore really didn't know how it stayed open, with the competition from the supermarket only one avenue over. But it was to the grocery store that her mother always sent her, insisted even that she patronize it. When she handed over the grocery bill receipt before emptying the family's worn but sturdy cloth shopping bag, Sore knew her mother was checking not just the cost of the items, but that she had gone to the appropriate store.

It wasn't that her parents knew Reb Khatskl, the owner, or that he had done anything in particular to warrant such loyalty. Her mother simply said, 'That's where we've always gone' or 'Cheaper isn't always better.' Sore knew the produce in this grocery store wasn't particularly fresh. The bananas and tomatoes sometimes had spots; the apples were regularly marred by brown circles and dents. If her mother noticed these, she never said a word, and Sore and her sisters knew better than to mention them. Of course, if the greens had bugs in it, they wouldn't be permitted to eat them. But bugs had never been found. Her father always certified them as safe for consumption, after checking them thoroughly against the kitchen overhead light fixture or in the natural light coming in the wonder above the sink, before her mother made the salad or soaked the cabbage for the sauerkraut. As Sore looked over at the plate glass window of Reb Khatskl's store, she could see the aisles of candy, even the same jelly beans and taffy ball pops that her sister Rivke used to pilfer. How she'd admired Rivke's fleetness of hand back then.

And then there were the stores on the avenue, whose names Sore knew but that remained unremarkable to her. There was an electronics store, selling all of the latest gadgets, adorned with posters in its front window blaring warnings in Hebrew and Yiddish against the internet, with its vast wellspring of pornography and lewdness. The biblical passage "Do not turn to follow your heart and eyes" crowned the posters in oversized block font. There was the toy store, with its array of bright, cheap playthings for children of all ages. Absently, Sore thought of the gift she still wished to purchase for her sister Leye's youngest, Meshulem. A rattle? A crib mobile? Something he could look up to on the way to and from sleep. There were so many other stores that Sore barely registered today, her day of return.

As she passed the glatt kosher Chinese take-out, the reason for this visit returned to Sore. Although she'd tried to convince herself that she was here for *Shvues*, Sore knew that wasn't the reason at all. Beyond the cheesecake and the blintzes and the flowers and rhododendron branches that adorned her family home, *Shvue*s never resonated with her as did the *Yomim Neroyim* and the other *Sholesh Regolim* of *Peysekh* and *Sukes*. This was the occasion when the *Bney-Yisroel* officially became *Am-Haseyfer*. Surely, there was no event of greater importance for her people. It was when men and boys stayed up all night to study, returning bleary-eyed but euphoric.

Sore knew that she too could have stayed up all night studying Torah and its commentaries (if not the Talmud proscribed to females) and that her parents probably would not have objected. Her father might even have been secretly pleased if she had done so. He was invariably proud of her scholastic achievements, the glowing report cards that she never failed to bring home. But Sore never asked her father for permission to stay up on *Shvues* night, not wishing to find out his answer. Better not to know than to be refused. Once Sore had slipped out to the great-aunt of her friend Mindl to watch *Yentl*. Perhaps like other girls in her world who had surreptitiously seen the film, she fleetingly saw herself as a scholar in drag, a veritable Barbra Streisand, if without the glorious vocal instrument. Yet just as Sore was no vegetarian neither was she a latter-day Yentl. And so *Shvues*, with its all-night Torah study and dairy diet and limits-never-tested, always seemed a bit pale to her.

Nearing her parents' home with the scraggly ginko tree in front of it, Sore had to admit, however reluctantly, that perhaps the Avenue hadn't changed at all. It was she who had changed, or rather her family that was on the brink of changing forever. In just a few days Rivke would be getting married. And that was why Sore, butterflies in her belly, was back on the Avenue, now walking up the stairs leading to her parents' rowhome. It was a change in herself, a reversion, from the woman she'd worked so hard to become, a woman without butterflies back to the sister, the daughter, perhaps even to the girl, who all lived all too uneasily with butterflies, who learned to co-exist with them, to elude the whirring of wings and the appearance of spots, the darting into diplomacy, or flight altogether.

***

Shvues had been fairly uneventful, and a bit disappointing without Leye and her family. Their absence wasn't a surprise. Before *yontef*, Sore had called to tell Leye that she was back in town. Leye said, 'I won't be coming by for an afternoon visit. Meshulem is colicky, and I don't want to take any chances and leave with him with Yudi, who'll be exhausted after staying up all night.' Sore had been looking forward to catching up with Leye but was able to hide her disappointment over the phone.

Almost as soon as she put down her luggage on *erev Shvues*, Sore took over from her mother with the cheesecake, still made with the graham cracker topping and crust. Sore didn't suggest fruit or chocolate for pizazz, the way she once had. With the blintzes, her mother would brook no assistance whatsoever. 'Just get ready for *yontef*, mamele,' she smiled.

Her father came back from the yeshiva, with a bouquet of roses, a whirl of red that he placed into the hands of his mother with a flourish, 'For my queen, my one and only.' Her mother threw back her head and laughed. Only her father caused her mother to laugh that way, in certainty, in abandon.

As her father dashed back out to the *mikve*, Sore started vacuuming and polishing the furniture, including her father's *shtender*. She used to imagine her own body, itself willowy and even boyish to this late day, hunched over the *shtender* late into the night after a Friday night winter meal, swaying with it to decipher a passage in Maimonides' *Mishneh Torah* or in pleasure over Rashi's insight on the weekly Torah portion.

The cheesecake, like the rest of the holiday fare, had turned out well. It was silky, not too sweet. Maybe her mother was right about this and everything else, Sore thought. The blintzes were exceptional, as expected. Her mother used almost no sugar in the cheese filling, allowing the creaminess within to come naturally to the fore. Her father brought along some yeshiva students for each of the main *Shvues* meals, a bit bleary-eyed but with great enthusiasm for the homemade cooking and generous in their compliments to her mother. Sore, thinking already about her dress, as yet unpurchased, for the upcoming wedding and the

50

eyes, including Rivke's, that would be assessing her, skipped the dairy delights altogether. Still, their appearance and the vocal approval of her father and his yeshiva students told her that the dairy dishes were indeed the culinary highlights of the meals.

The mood at the lesser meals, when there were no students, was optimistic, hopeful even. Her mother said that the groom Avigdor was his name (and here Sore thought again of *Yentl*) came from an *erlekhe mishpokhe*. They were active in some kind of import and export business. Her mother couldn't recall exactly what it was when Sore pressed her for more information.

'You could've found out more if you came to the *vort*,' her mother said.

'But Ma, you know I had to some fundraising, and we had to look at the new seminary building plans that were due soon after that. I just couldn't take the time off,' Sore responded to her mother's pooh-poohing, having made the same argument to the same effect months prior.

'In any case, Avigdor's *mishpokhe* has supported our yeshiva for many years,' her father inserted.

And if Avigdor was both once divorced and quite a bit older than Rivke, well, Rivke at thirty-three was no youngster herself. Sore expertly deflected attention from what was sure to be the next topic of conversation – her own age, considerably beyond that of Rivke's – by stating that she was so happy for her sister and looked forward to meeting the groom. Her mother's eyes met hers in a shrewd and knowing glance.

***

The next day, after they'd cleared away the *Shvues* dishes the only time such fine porcelain was used for dairy meals Sore and her mother headed out to the dressmaker's shop. Located on the same avenue as the supermarket never frequented by Sore and her mother, the shop catered to the varying needs of the community. Although the name of the store was The Bridal Boutique, it was really so much more. Everyone said so. The ladies from the community went there to get ready for all of their *simkhes*. The store had every size and style imaginable but all with low hems, long sleeves, and high necklines as mandated by rabbinical specifications. This meant the ladies didn't have to sort through (or be tempted by) any immodest clothing. And Mrs. Silverstein, the owner, and her staff could have alterations completed in no time if warranted.

'*Brukhim ha-boim*, *Rebetsin* and Sorele!' Mrs. Silverstein called out as they entered to the accompaniment of a bell chime fastened to the door. Sore shuddered at hearing the diminutive form of her name. When had she last been called that? Even her father, with his bursts of affection, hadn't called her that in years. Although she had been dreading this shopping excursion, Sore's arm tightened around her mother's. Sore was grateful for her mother's companionship; she didn't think she could've faced Mrs. Silverstein on her own.

That support proved to be short-lived. While her mother was drawn to the black and navy (midnight?) blue dresses, Sore was drawn to the pinks and reds. So what if she were the assistant head mistress at a women's teachers' seminary in the middle of the country? This was her remaining sister's wedding, and for once she was going to let go a little.

'This pink is too young, and the red – *Es past nisht*. You can't wear red to your sister's wedding,' her mother asserted.

'Why? Rivke, of all people, won't care. She'd love it if I did. She'd wish she could wear it', Sore responded.

'Rivke is not the girl, I mean the woman, she once was. She fell in with some people that she shouldn't have been with. But that was years ago. Now she's on the right track. You'll see.'

Sore marveled at her mother's vague yet decidedly glib appraisal of Rivke's thirteen years of disreputable living after dropping out of seminary. Even now, right before Rivke's wedding, she couldn't say that Rivke fell in with a really bad crowd. No mention of the really shady men, all seen in secret, in another borough. Of course, everyone in the neighborhood found out. And no mention either of the fact that Rivke couldn't seem to hold down a job. Even certain receptionist ones that didn't require clerical skills. Rivke couldn't master transferring a telephone call or smiling at guests. God only knew what substances had fried her brain and what travails and tribulations kept her in a state of suspicion bordering on paranoia, even to strangers coming in to a bargain basement car rental or auto shop. How Rivke would manage to smile at the camera in a few days, Sore had no idea. There was no mention of the "loans" that Rivke had begged from her mother until she stopped giving. And, of course, there was no mention of the "loans" she asked of Sore, who couldn't stop giving. Of course she knew her mother wouldn't mention these things. Her mother never mentioned the money she gave Rivke, and Sore never told her mother (or anyone else) of the money she too had given Rivke. Sore was certain that Rivke never paid her mother back, just as she never paid Sore back. And besides, here they were in The Bridal Boutique only a few days before Rivke's big event. Sore hated that these unholy thoughts were clouding her mind at this moment, but there they were.

Somewhere between the dark hues preferred by her mother and the pinks and reds that Sore wanted, they settled on some gray and lavender options. Her mother followed Sore into the dressing room, insisting that there was no point in her sitting outside on the row of velvet chairs positioned outside. 'Besides you'll need my help with the buttons and the zipper,' her mother added.

Under the fluorescent glare of the dressing room light, mother and daughter appraised the daughter's form, down to bra and panties. Sore was even tempted to remove those. Only she didn't. There was no need to. The lines and curves to be assessed in relation to the dress were all too apparent. And besides, she didn't really even need a bra. Sore wondered why she bothered to buy them at all. Perhaps it was in homage to the occasion not unlike this one when her mother had gone with her to purchase her first bra in the city. Had her mother done the same with Rivke? With Leye? Probably not or they would have told her. Rivke would certainly have told her. Rivke, with cigarette in hand, after Beys-Yankev, laughing at the very notion of modesty, exhaling rings of smoke into the schoolyard, would have said something. Sore remembered those many afternoons, as Rivke chatted about her crisis of the moment, savoring her nicotine fix, while she, Sore, anxiously looked around, keeping an eye out for the principal or some of the gossipy girls.

'Look how flat I am. There's nothing drooping because there's nothing *to* droop.'

'Flat! Nonsense! You look gorgeous. Girls half your age would be jealous of such a figure,' her mother replied.

After Sore tried on two rather funereal numbers, they agreed on the suitability of an "ashes of rose" creation. It had some of the pink hue that Sore wanted and yet was respectable enough to earn her mother's approval. She saw in its shade the colors that were printed on the outside of the pages of her well-thumbed edition of the *Mikroyes Gedoyles* she'd studied for years, mastered even, dazzling her teachers over the years with her diligence and her originality. 'If only … ' Mrs. Shifman, her fifth grade teacher, had once said, or started to say when she saw Sore studying late after school one day. 'If only you had been a boy,' her seventh grade teacher Mrs. Frank, living up to her name, had more bluntly stated. This was the same edition of the *Mikroyes Gedoyles* Sore used when teaching her students and that she used now when called away from her administrative duties to deliver to the students a *devar* Torah or a *shier-khizek*. Sore won the set as a prize for the highest grade point average in Torah study and for best overall *mides*.

And now, clad in this high-collared and long, very long-sleeved dress, a compromise between her mother and herself, a dress that neither of them wanted nor were particularly fond of, the thought of her *Mikroyes Gedoyles* somehow made this purchase palatable, worthwhile even. Worthwhile for herself, worthwhile for the vision of the three sisters, in roles they no longer knew, poised for the wedding camera's snap. Her father called them the Three Matriarchs, even though there were, of course, Four of Them in the Torah. Only the matriarch Rokhl was absent. Of course, her parents had insisted that they were named after deceased relatives, as was the custom, as was right. It just happened that way, her mother often said. But Sore suspected the daughters were named after an abstract idea in her father's imagination, a manifestation of feminine wisdom and unity. As a girl, Sore always wondered if their fates would at least partially mirror those of the biblical Matriarchs. Would a son born to Sore in old age be brought to sacrifice? Would Rivke have two sons one outdoorsy and hairy and … the other a man of the Book, an *ish tam yoshev oholim*? Would Leye be forced to wait for the man she loved, the one who didn't, in the end, really love her as much as he did another? When Leye married and appeared to have found contentment (even though everyone said the heartthrob Yudi would break Leye's), Sore breathed an inward sigh of relief at her own chances. Perhaps Sore would escape the First Matriarch's fate. Perhaps the Torah had loosened its grip across the millennia, after all.

Sore wished suddenly that she could chuckle with Leye over the day and this dressing room in The Bridal Boutique presided over by Mrs. Silverstein. Only it'd been so long since she could do that with Leye since she married young (at the right time) and had so many children and could never find the time for Sore, try as she might. Leye was the righteous one, who fulfilled her duty to her parents as a daughter and to the people of Israel as a woman, something that she, Sore, with her Torah and *hasmodeh*, had never done.

As she stared at her body and the ashes of rose dress carefully hanging on the "Must Have!" hook in the dressing room and thought of her mother now waiting outside, Sore wondered how she would go forward in just a few days. How would she find the strength to meet the pitying stares (*Im yirtseshem bay dir*) or the blank neutrality of the more discreet women?

And even though Sore knew that no one, let alone an assistant principal of a teachers' seminary, should be so petty, she couldn't help asking herself the following: How would she forget the many thousands of dollars she "lent" to Rivke, spent on who knows what, and never repaid, never considered important enough to be repaid or even worthy of excuses for not repaying? How could she forgive Rivke's ignoring all of her advice, despite repeating seeking of said advice? How could she forgive Rivke (and their parents?) for completely excluding her from the wedding planning? How could she forgive Rivke for never telling her about her engagement to this man, this soon-to-be-husband, this Avigdor, with whom Rivke would soon be sharing her life? How could she forgive this Avigdor for robbing her of her Rivke? Yes, the Rivke who smoked in the *Beys-Yankev* courtyard while Sore looked anxiously around. Yes, the Rivke of the questionable judgment and the terrible choices who despite all, was her most beloved, the one closest to her, the one who listened to the triumphs of her academic prizes and the disinterested responses and outright rejections from the suitors conveyed to Sore by the *shadkhonim* both on the Avenue and beyond.

Opening the dressing room door, dressed now in her quotidian assistant principal's dress and jacket, the new dress over her arm, she saw her mother waiting, but not expectantly as Sore had imagined. She was looking away, lost in reflection of her own, until she realized – after Sore had been standing in silence watching – that Sore was ready to pay. And as her mother finally rose towards her, offering to help carry something, at least the new dress slip, Sore knew that when the glass was shattered under the wedding canopy, she would be standing nearby, in this ashes of rose dress. However much she wanted to, Sore couldn't and wouldn't wriggle out of this obligation, this magnetic field. She would be there in celebration of Rivke's joy late discovered. She would be there with Leye and her brood alongside. How many children did Leye and Yudi have now? Seven? Eight? She would be there with her parents, aging, beaming.

As the dancing started, as cries of "Mazl tov!" resounded through the hall, Sore would be there, planning her next *shier-khizek* for the teachers' seminary students. A volume of her *Mikroyes Gedoyles* would be in her handbag in the cloakroom. She would ask the attendant to retrieve it for her. She would open it if she needed a respite from the festivities. Its words, the ashes of rose pattern visible, not on an individual page, but only from the side when the book in its totality as a sacred object was viewed, would carry her to the wedding's end.

"Flowers for Madame"

When Beyle entered her room, she was pleased by its high ceilings and tall windows, as well as its distance from the bustle of the village square. There was a double bed and plenty of closet space, she noticed as she stepped further from the door. Beyle liked to walk around a room when she first entered it, especially one in which she was planning to spend a considerable amount of time. You really could tell so much about a space by moving through it, instead of just glancing around at it. Beyle did not claim (to herself or to others) to be an expert in feng-shui, but she knew she had to feel comfortable with the energy points and flow throughout a room.

Her daughter Freydl reserved the rooms in this inn several weeks ago. Freydl assured Beyle not to worry about the payment; they could figure all that out later. Beyle was pleased that Freydl's room would not adjoin her own; its precise location would be determined only after Freydl's arrival. Originally, Freydl wanted her own room to be near her mother's; she thought the proximity would be great fun, especially following a night on the town. But Beyle managed to get Freydl to agree to rent a room further down the corridor. She hoped Freydl would follow through on that commitment. Beyle really did need her privacy, and Freydl needed hers, too. Or so Beyle imagined, although Freydl had not mentioned anything about privacy or a need for it.

Beyle began to hang up her clothes, mostly light summer dresses, along with a few shawls and sweaters in the wardrobe. She'd packed lightly for this trip, or at least not as elaborately as she usually packed. This was to be a visit with few social obligations; in fact, no one knew either of them here. Freydl, who had lived abroad several times, seemed to know people in many of the main global tourist destinations or she knew people who knew people who could provide introductions for them. It was always fun to meet other people, but sometimes Beyle just wanted to enjoy the holiday quietly, away from her pressure-filled position as an administrative assistant at a downtown financial firm. Traveling with her daughter could be simultaneously stressful and exhilarating.

After putting her clothes away in the wardrobe, Beyle ran her hands over the surface. It was constructed solidly of oak, and the carving of a diamond motif in the corner was exquisite. It all appeared to be hand-done, as did the border tiles in the terra cotta floor of the room itself. Someone had taken care with the room's overall design and furnishings.

Beyle was glad they weren't staying in a modern hotel with all the amenities and creature comforts. Of course, she liked to work out on the stationary bike or the treadmill in the morning and lifting light dumbbells every other day had eliminated much of the flab on her upper arms. But Beyle wanted this trip to be different, truly restful and away from the touristy areas, completely off the proverbial beaten path. And this inn, at least at this early stage of the visit, seemed to be exactly what Beyle wanted. It was relatively small and located in a remote region. In fact, the driver from the airport was surprised when she informed him of her destination. She wasn't even sure he knew the route. The bumpy ride over unpaved roads did little to reassure her. It was only when he pulled up in front of the inn, which she recognized from the photographs that Beyle could truly relax. And relax she would!

A sense of tranquility now pervaded Beyle. Already she felt herself transformed by a wellness of being. Her meridians felt open to her; her chi centers in alignment. A breeze stirred the sheer curtains at the window. The late afternoon sun bathed the mustard-painted room in a golden-brown glow. She smiled, imagining herself to be situated inside one of the fried potato blintzes she used to make for her family so many years ago and which she desperately tried to avoid making in these waistline-watching days of late. Strange that such an image would come to her here, so far from home and when she was already feeling so relaxed. She would take a lavender-infused bath now. Surely, that would dispel the carb-and-starch images.

***

Mother and daughter met for dinner in the dining room just to the left of the inn's lobby. Freydl hadn't realized how far the village was from the airport or she would have arranged for them to ride together. Her ride over was just as bumpy as Beyle's, even if it wasn't as unexpected a tourist destination to *her* driver. Freydl looked quite travel-weary in contrast to her own refreshed self. There was an air of fatigue about her. Clearly, she hadn't changed from her travel clothes; Beyle wondered if she'd even taken a shower or a bath. Additionally, there were bags under her eyes and her curly hair, usually so carefully shaped, hung limply about her puffy cheeks. And had Freydl put on more weight? Beyle felt that when one traveled abroad, one was representing country, not simply self or family or community. As such, one always needed to conduct one's self accordingly. Beyle saw herself as an emissary, bringing forth good will and an eagerness to learn and share. Perhaps that was a bit self-important and grandiose, but that was how Beyle felt.

That new girlfriend of Freydl's was clearly not good for her, Beyle thought. The one time that Beyle met her didn't go well, to say the least. Beyle found the girlfriend to be unpleasant and controlling, dominating the conversation with "meaningful" glances and prolonged silence. What was her name? Sue? Syb? Sal? It was definitely one of those two-syllable "S" names with one syllable chopped off. Did it really expend that much more energy to say Susan or Sybil or Sally? Did the shortened form convey a greater intimacy? Beyle tended to think not. She, for one, had never been tempted to call her daughter "Frey".

Beyle remembered how relieved she felt when Freydl came out as a lesbian. Now, Beyle would no longer be the principal scandalous figure in the family. But her relief turned to concern and then unease over the years. Freydl's choices in women really weren't up to par. Sue/Syb/Sal was just the most recent in a long line of ne'er-do-wells that Freydl dated, each more marginal, or even derelict, than the previous one. One of them made a scene sulking and shouting after Beyle asked her to smoke outside after dinner. Despite repeated scrubbing, that cigarette stain never did come out of the taupe Berber carpet, a talisman of an unpleasant evening and a cautionary note against poor life choices. Beyle caught herself slipping into an appraisal of her daughter's presentation of self and her life decisions and arranged her mouth in what she hoped was an accepting smile and removed the crease in her brow that conveyed her displeasure or worry.

The meal of lamb and grilled vegetables was delicious. Wherever they traveled, Beyle and Freydl liked to order separate dishes so that each could taste the other's food. Here, however, there was no menu at all, and the meal they were now eating was the only one offered. Beyle only experienced this once before, when she went hiking with a friend in the mountains not long after her divorce. They stayed overnight at a similarly remote inn. Only there, the food was heavily fried and fatty. Despite the appetite she worked up from hiking, Beyle was able to avoid the bacon and sausages in that mountain inn dining room, even as she wondered if the dishes she *was* consuming were cooked in pig fat. Ravenous, she wasn't able to bring herself to ask. Here, she had no such fears. The food was delicious and clearly quite healthy.

Freydl seemed equally pleased with her meal. She devoured the contents of the plate even more quickly than Beyle, only nodding her head in assent at her mother's exclamations of "delicious!" and "mmm". Freydl hadn't always had such a robust appetite or frame. In the months leading up to her parents' divorce, she ate less and less. With the drama of the divorce consuming her, Freydl was for Beyle an ever-diminishing waif at the corner of her mind's eye.

If, years later, the divorce seemed inevitable, that was certainly not the case at the time. A matchmaker had brokered the match between Shiye and Beyle with little fanfare, and the match back then was considered quite successful. Beyle learned after the wedding that the matchmaker even boasted about it to some of her friends in the neighborhood. They only went on three dates prior to the engagement, and these were conducted in the dim lounge of a hotel. Beyle had just turned eighteen and barely knew what to ask Shiye. Her conversation with men up to that point was strictly limited to a few relatives, mostly her brother, Izzy and her father, who spoke very little with her or her mother or any other females, for that matter. "*Al tarbeh siḥah 'im ishah*" was the Talmudic dictum that governed her father's relations with the opposite sex. Her mother gave her a bit of coaching beforehand about suitable topics of conversation with Shiye.

And yet the conversation between Beyle and Shiye flowed quite smoothly. They spoke of their studies, their dreams of living a year in the Holy Land, and of raising children in a household steeped in love of Torah and in awe of God. They also talked about the city's professional baseball team streaking to a pennant at the time and their favorite flavors of ice cream (hers: mint chocolate chip; his: jamoca almond fudge), among other lighter topics.

When Beyle found herself under the *khupe* less than a year later, she wasn't at all surprised. This was what she'd always wanted. She knew herself to be radiant beneath the veil and the two of them to be a handsome couple. She still remembered the matchmaker's name: Mrs. Nissenson. Mrs. Malke Nissenson.

Freydl asked to be excused from an evening stroll, citing her exhaustion from the long trip. She'd kept her promise of reserving a room that did not adjoin her mother's and seemed quite content, almost eager, to retire there for the evening.

Walking alone from the hotel to the village square, Beyle was enchanted by the clarity of the night sky. The stars were sharply outlined; the moon nearly fully formed. Still, Beyle had to look down regularly to determine where to place her feet. The narrow winding streets of the village were paved with cobblestones, some jutting at unusual angles. She admired their charm and impracticality and wondered how the villagers lived with them all their lives. Beyle was glad she was wearing sensible espadrilles and not the high heels which showed off her ankles, still slim at age sixty-one.

A bench in the town square, not far from the central fountain, proved to be an ideal location for an evening reverie. Once again, Beyle was pleased with the distance of her room and the inn from the square. She was surprised that the square was so busy at this hour. She saw couples of all ages walking along the square and then down the tree-lined avenues into the village. There were quite a few cafes lining the square, nearly all filled. Beyle heard laughter and phrases and snippets of conversation, occasionally catching a familiar word or phrase. There didn't appear to be many tourists seated. Although she was only a few feet away from the cafes, Beyle felt a chasm unfold between herself and the conversation and laughter. This, then, was the paradox of the tourist, she thought: yearning to be a part of the "authentic" local experience yet necessarily unable to partake.

'Flowers for Madame?'

This question jolted Beyle out of her dour musings. A young man she judged to be in his early thirties, a good ten years younger than Freydl, spoke these words. Ordinarily, Beyle would shake her head "no" at such a request, but there was something about the slightly melancholy evening and the young man himself that led her to nod rather emphatically. She didn't find him attractive, at least not conventionally so. His hair was cut very short, almost military in style, and his frame was rather lanky. Beyle preferred her men somewhat more zaftig. Shiye, even in his youth had a naturally husky frame. But this man's eyes were so lively, and his smile was so winning in the lamplight of the square. Beyle found herself smiling in return and pointing to white roses in the young man's cane basket.

After they completed the sale, the young man offered observations about the night that was so bright and the air that was so fresh. Beyle nodded in agreement, noting his pattern of speech, slow and searching, not fluent exactly but not broken either. Beyle allowed him to search for the words, restraining herself from supplying them in her language, as she normally did when speaking with locals while on holiday.

They each introduced each other after the brief exchange. His name was Immanuel. Beyle usually introduced herself as Bella, but for the second time in this brief encounter, she decided to go against her precedent. She carefully sounded out the pronunciation and then listened to him repeat it several times. She waited for the predictable, fawning comment about how she lived up to her name. Only it never came. After mastering the pronunciation, Immanuel bowed slightly and withdrew. Beyle watched him walk by other tables, complete several additional transactions, and then disappear around the bend from view.

***

The next day was quite eventful. After an early hearty breakfast, Beyle and Freydl left the hotel on their first hiking expedition. The concierge and the head waiter warned each of them separately as they came downstairs of the extreme heat predicted in the forecast. Both wanted to hike as much as they could before the sun was at its peak. Beyle was surprised and pleased by Freydl's eagerness.

Freydl ran a small spa that specialized in Swedish massage techniques and cleansing facials. Booking the clients, verifying that the supplies were on hand, and keeping the clients content kept Freydl busy six, sometimes seven days a week. As it turned out, the relaxation business was really stressful. Freydl tried to hire an assistant/receptionist, but they turned out to be more harm than help. They could never keep the booking schedules in order, regularly double booking some of her most popular masseuses. Freydl found it easier to do the work herself than delegate it to others. With so much pressure at work, Freydl had said she wanted a vacation where she could just lie around in the sun, read some mysteries or doze. But just as she'd agreed to her mother's request for an out-of-the way hotel, so too did Freydl agree to a hike on the first day. Beyle knew she was taking Freydl away from lying around in the sun, but she was glad to have the chance to catch up with her.

The two exchanged gossip about their office while taking in the rugged if unspectacular mountain scenery of scrub brush and desert foliage. At least, Beyle thought, this could be considered desert. Maybe it was considered semi-desert or just an arid climate? In any case, dust was everywhere; Beyle felt it seeping in her hiking shoes. And they really were shoes made for hiking – not gym sneakers and not hiking boots. Beyle was pleased by their stylishness and practicality. Freydl also felt sand seeping into her boots and suggested that they stop every now and again to shake it out.

Freydl's spa was doing reasonably well. But because of the competitiveness of the field, Freydl had to find new methods of increasing her visibility. The conventional methods of advertising seemed to have yielded few results. As an administrative assistant, Beyle's life was less uncertain and dramatic, but she enjoyed describing the various office personalities and their foibles and the occasional office romances, rather than the work itself. Sure, she embellished the receptionist's gum chewing or the occasional touching she saw between several analysts at lunch or in the hallway. She had to keep Freydl's attention. And Freydl did seem genuinely interested.

Beyle was enjoying her time with Freydl and, in fact, had enjoyed their get-togethers for these many years since her divorce from Shiye. It had taken them years to reach this state of even communication. The divorce was particularly volcanic, although the path leading up to it was slow and uneven. Beyle couldn't pinpoint a day when she felt particularly distant from her affectionate husband. Sometimes, she looked at around the dining room table on Shabbas and reminded herself how much she did have: a wonderful husband, healthy, contented children, and a comfortable home. But she was running through a checklist in her mind. During the workweek, she felt stifled in her role as mother to Freydl and her youngest, Dov-Ber. The routine of cleaning, cooking, mending, and tending no longer seemed enough. She felt at once restless and listless, edgy and enervated. Was this all there would ever be for her?

And why was she like this? Beyle came from a prominent, devout family. There wasn't a tradition of rebellion in her carefully traced lineage. Beyle noted this in a family tree project she'd completed years before. The genealogical work was a source of great pride to Beyle. She took great care with it, looking up the spellings of the shtetlach, or small towns, of her forebears, finding the titles and publication information of the books of the rabbis. She even interviewed relatives, who shared anecdotes and lore passed down through the generations. If there had been rebels, surely she would have heard of them. The women in the family had not shied away from gossip before. So why this unease?

Shiye refused to allow Beyle to explore the possibility of salaried employment. He didn't want his wife to work outside the home, although many women in the community did just that. There was no *halakhic* prohibition or even rabbinical injunction against it. Beyle asked the rabbi directly for permission during one of their numerous meetings with him, but he never gave a direct answer. Was he in cahoots with Shiye? She returned from these meetings trembling in rage and blasted Shiye for his small-mindedness. His responses of 'Don't I provide you with everything you need?' and 'How can you be so ungrateful?' only further fueled her fury. Beyle was grateful to Shiye for his hard work and success in the diamond industry, but her very life force was draining from her in the subdued, pious comfort of their home. After one such exchange, Beyle threw dishes and cups at Shiye. He easily ducked them and left the kitchen, ushering out Freydl and Dov-Ber who had been staring from the shadows of the hallway, transfixed by the meltdown. Afterwards, Beyle bent over the shards of crockery on the floor, sobbing in despair.

The children were split up between the parents. Freydl was a high school senior and chose to finish out the school year at *Beys-Yankev*. She moved with her mother out of the neighborhood and commuted back in for school. Other than her considerable weight loss, the divorce had little observable effect on Freydl. In fact, she only seemed more driven to succeed. She was third in her class and earned a full scholarship to an elite, private college up North. Dov-Ber refused to speak to Beyle for years, and even to this day, maintained only a frosty connection with her. At his own wedding, he asked Shiye's new wife to walk him, alongside Shiye, down the aisle. Beyle seethed unaccompanied in a corner of the room since Freydl was sitting with other relatives. Dov-Ber's children accepted her gifts and overtures these days with politeness and disinterest. She was sure the gifts were quickly discarded, but she nevertheless felt obligated to give them.

After they got back to the inn from their hike, Freydl went up to her room for a brief nap. She wanted to rest and then sit by the tiled pool in the back courtyard. Beyle returned to the village square, curious to compare its daytime rhythms. She randomly selected one of the cafes and ordered an iced coffee, which was delicious. Today, Beyle was not startled by Immanuel since he appeared before her in the distance and then approached, smiling. She invited him to join her for a coffee. Immanuel didn't drink coffee but ordered an iced mineral water. The two sat in silence, surprised in its comfort since they barely knew each other. Beyle noticed the word "two" in her thoughts and thought about the proximity and distance of the word "two" to the words "both" or "couple". Of course, they were "two" and not a couple. And yet she found herself drawn by his ease and understatement, and his ready smile, not mysterious or pointedly charming, but somehow content, pleased to see and be with her. After Beyle paid for the refreshment, Immanuel walked with her back to the inn.

As the days drifted by, Beyle looked forward to seeing Immanuel. They never made plans to meet exactly. Whenever she stopped in the square, Immanuel would somehow always be there or rather, would arrive shortly after her. Was he looking out for her arrival? Beyle assumed he was but never asked. He always joined her, sometimes drinking iced mineral water, sometimes sitting with her in their companionable quiet that was in such marked contrast to the volubility she shared with her daughter.

Occasionally, when walking through the village's hilly, twisted alleys and streets, Beyle heard footsteps behind her or saw Immanuel appear ahead. He came to walk alongside during these jaunts, never trying to take her hand or link her arm in his. There was never any question of getting truly "lost"; the village was too small for that. But Beyle appreciated the company, the sureness with which he navigated the hills and turns. When she stopped to admire bright red flowers in a pot outside a window or a door, Immanuel smiled at her enjoyment.

Beyle knew from their first evening that Immanuel's verbal skills were quite good. However, she found herself so relaxed, so at peace with him in their wordlessness. She knew she was headed into the realm of fantasy, a problematic one at that: the romanticized native, the colonized, mysterious "other". She had had enough conversations with Freydl over the years and browsed enough of Freydl's college and then graduate texts on post-colonial and feminist theory to become familiar with the tropes and language. "Trendy jargon", Freydl now labeled it dismissively. Still, Beyle didn't want to disrupt the mood they created with self-conscious, "constructed" silence or even minimal words. Rather, she sought and found herself in a state between silence and words, one of peace and ease.

One afternoon in the square, Beyle invited Immanuel to join them at the inn for dinner. Freydl had inquired about the nature of her mother's walks, and once even suggested jokingly that she would follow her mother one day. And so Beyle decided that introductions were in order. Immanuel readily consented. Beyle left a note under Freydl's door letting her know that they'd be joined by another at dinner tonight. She likewise informed the concierge. She didn't want Immanuel's presence to surprise anyone.

Immanuel was already waiting when Beyle arrived several minutes early in the lobby. They sat themselves in the dining room waiting for Freydl. As the minutes ticked away, Beyle found herself touching her hair absently, anxious for the evening to go well. Beyle told herself that her concern was unfounded. She simply invited a pleasant man to dinner with her daughter and herself. Freydl couldn't fail to be as charmed with Immanuel as she was. Freydl arrived and immediately apologized for her tardiness.

The dinner went well. Freydl managed to draw Immanuel out in conversation in a light, convivial manner. As it turned out, Immanuel came from a large family. His father was in the municipal civil service; his mother was a baker by profession. Most of his siblings had moved away, seeking the greater opportunities of the city. Immanuel preferred the slower pace of the village and wanted to remain close to the family, particularly to look after his mother, who had a bad heart. Beyle marveled both at the dexterity with which Freydl elicited these personal details without appearing to be fishing for information and at Immanuel's ease of response. In just one evening, she learned more about Immanuel's background than on the numerous occasions she'd spent with him.

After dinner, Immanuel excused himself and left the inn. Beyle went back to her room to bask in the success of the evening and prepare for bed. In her nightgown, she was surprised to hear a knock on the door. Freydl entered without Beyle's permission and immediately launched into a tirade:

'Ma, what are you doing with this guy? He's half your age! Are you completely out of your mind? This is who you've been "seeing" on your afternoon walks? Can't you see he's after something? That he's playing you? Or do you think you can just suddenly make yourself into a "cougar"? You think you can control this situation?'

'I'm surprised to hear you say this, Freydl. I thought the evening went well. You seemed to like him. What exactly do you think he's after? What is it that I "have" that he "wants"? Certainly, it isn't my money. You know very well there isn't much of that.'

'I don't know. But I won't have you made into a laughingstock. This is outrageous.'

'Freydl, you've said enough. Why don't you get some sleep, darling? Let's discuss this in the morning.'

Drifting off to sleep, Beyle felt she'd handled Freydl's outrage as best she could. She hadn't said anything she'd regret the next day, anything about Freydl's jealousy of the men in her life since the divorce, always finding something inappropriate in them – too old, too young, too rich, too poor, too effeminate. There were so many reasons why such and such suitor wasn't good enough for her sexy, eligible mother. Why should tonight and Immanuel have been any different? Cougar?! Really? Beyle dismissed such claims as predictable and obvious, not worthy of the rigourously trained mind of her daughter and the bond they worked so hard to repair and develop since the crockery and her marriage shattered on the kitchen floor so long ago. Suddenly,

Beyle remembered how she once quipped to Freydl, after they both moved away from Shiye and Dov-Ber, that her marriage was bookended by glass shards at the *khupe* and crockery on the kitchen floor leading to the divorce.

Breakfast the next morning was tense. Freydl ate her eggs with barely a "good morning" nod at her mother and quickly left the table. Beyle finished her breakfast alone and exited the inn, determined not to let Freydl's outburst and moodiness spoil her day or otherwise get the best of her. She began her climb up the mountain trails that she and Freydl had regularly hiked together. She was surprised when Immanuel asked if he could join her when she was about ten minutes into the hike. She wasn't surprised by Immanuel's appearance, of course, but he'd never appeared here on the mountain trails. Of course, she'd never walked alone on the trails, either, she realized.

Their walk continued quietly along. Beyle was sweating more than usual. When she realized Immanuel was leading her on an unfamiliar route, she wondered if the hike was more arduous. They still had to stop periodically so Beyle could remove the dust and sand from her shoes. Immanuel didn't seem to mind it in his shoes, or perhaps there was none. Did he know of a way to keep the sand out of shoes? Was the day just hotter? After an hour, Immanuel stopped Beyle and kissed her for the first time. Deeply, passionately, although with his hands at his sides. Beyle responded with equal depth and passion. In this unfamiliar landscape, her response felt complete, without restraint.

In her room at the inn, Immanuel's skills at lovemaking appeared almost mathematical in their precision. He kissed her body as if knowing her most sensitive points even before her moans confirmed his intuition – just below her nipples, between her breasts, her armpits, the nape of her neck. Instead of feeling awkward and bloated next to Immanuel's slimness, Beyle rejoiced in him, alive to his body's agility and electricity. She always preferred to be weighed down by men, to be enveloped by their size. Here, she felt herself open, vulnerable in her pleasure.

The next day passed in a blur. Beyle invited Freydl to afternoon tea, hoping the two of them could come to some sort of understanding. She didn't care about the appearance of things or what anyone thought. She just couldn't bear the tension between herself and Freydl. Only, it was no use.

Beyle saw the verdict of herself reflected back at her from Freydl's eyes. A gigolo on the move some thirty years her mother's junior had unhinged her, and she, Freydl, couldn't seem to stop it. But Beyle knew it was more than that. Here was her mother – the archetypal westerner unbalanced by the sun and white stucco and dust of the holiday. This figure was the floppy underbelly of the efficient colonizer, the one who failed to make do in the brightness of the colonized realm. She had deliberately strayed too far, had taken the next step in the tourist's natural tendency to romanticization of the native, to something altogether unseemly. Beyle saw all this in Freydl's eyes, in the disgust that hadn't left Freydl's face since her outburst to Beyle after the dinner with Immanuel. Beyle wondered if a Jew could be considered the "archetypal westerner" when so much anti-Semitic rhetoric over the years considered them the "easterner" or "Oriental" or just the "other". She found herself getting lost in reflections on discourses with which she had only a passing acquaintance but which had somehow etched themselves into her mind. In any case, the tea was a disaster.

The next morning Beyle saw Freydl, her packed bags beside her, speaking to the clerk at the front desk. She was finalizing her bill and checking out of the inn four days earlier than they planned. Beyle did not rush forward to try and stop her or even speak with her. She wanted to see if Freydl would notice her and reach out. But Freydl didn't. As soon as the bill was settled, Freydl wheeled her luggage out to the waiting taxi. As Freydl entered the taxi, the luggage was quickly loaded in. The taxi sped away. Beyle wondered if Freydl gave a backward glance at the inn and the holiday they planned with such excitement for months.

***

With Freydl gone, Beyle's bond with Immanuel deepened. She called the airline to cancel her return flight. She called her supervisor Mr. Maitland to ask for an extension on her holiday, for leave without pay.

'There are some things I have to take care of, matters to arrange,' she said.

'How long do you need exactly, Beyle? There is a new round of contract negotiations coming up. We really need you here.'

'I'm not yet sure. Would four months be OK?'

'Four months? That long?'

'I'm afraid so. I really need this time.'

'Well, OK. I'll put a note in your file and let HR know. But this can't be indefinite. We can't hold your position forever. I'm only doing this because you've been such an outstanding employee.'

'Thank you so much, Mr. Maitland. I am forever grateful to you for this opportunity. You won't regret it.'

After hanging up the telephone, Beyle felt a sense of calm and relief. She was relieved Mr. Maitland hadn't asked her where she was or what she was doing. How could she have explained any of this? And yet nothing felt rash or unplanned. In fact, she felt her natural tendency to plan – the very tendency that had planned this nearly flawless holiday to perfection – take over. This was, after all, what made her valuable enough to Mr. Maitland (and her colleagues) that he would allow her this rarely granted leave without pay status. Beyle knew they could easily have let her go (she hated to use the word "fire" with herself or others in the firm). There were plenty of others, far younger and more technologically savvy than herself, who would've happily taken the position. Who knows? They still might; Beyle couldn't think about that at this point.

That same day, she checked out of the inn and rented a studio apartment three streets from the central village square where she first met Immanuel. The kitchen was small but well-stocked with pots and pans and cooking utensils. Beyle cooked meals for Immanuel, learning to master the local ingredients – the rice, beans, chicken and the various spices and flavorings. She spent most of her mornings browsing through the market just off the square. Sometimes he suggested dishes or ingredients, and occasionally, ways to improve her cooking. Beyle happily absorbed his feedback, surprised by her lack of defensiveness.

Afterwards they would slip, fall, or otherwise descend into Beyle's bed. Their lovemaking remained elaborate, choreographed by an invisible hand. Beyle was surprised at Immanuel's moves, his sleight of hand never revealed until it was felt on her body. She never asked him about his previous lovers, presumably the sources of education for this expertise, just as he never asked her about Shiye or the men that followed him.

Even if Beyle continued to reject terms such as "madness" or "spell" that Freydl used or suggested, she did begin to lose sense of time. The days fell into a rhythm every bit as pleasurable as her nights. She loved the market, the brightness of its colors, and the richness of its fruit. The flowers called out to her; she always made sure to bring some home with her. Immanuel could've brought unsold flowers home to her but she preferred to purchase the ones in the market. These were less obviously "romantic", bunched together in complementary variety and texture. She never thought to ask their names, although they were different from the flowers she knew back at home. Never had she eaten, breathed or seen so powerfully in such full measure.

Immanuel asked nothing of her. He continued to work as a flower vendor and to help his mother with her baked goods business. Not pies, exactly, but something like them, Beyle gathered. She was never quite sure. She wasn't invited to meet any members of Immanuel's family, and she never requested an invitation. Immanuel never asked Beyle for money as Freydl had so crassly suggested. At night, he sought only to pleasure her, his release coming only after her own satisfaction. Immanuel invariably left the studio apartment before dawn, sometimes earlier. Beyle had never experienced a liaison, a connection so effortless, one that asked so little of her and gave her so much. Everything, she began to feel.

***

The days bled into weeks, and then months. Beyle had long since passed the four months leave-without-pay period granted by Mr. Maitland. She never called Mr. Maitland to let him know her decision not to return or even her whereabouts. What did any of that previous life matter now? Occasionally, while walking through the lanes of the market, the thought that Immanuel might be in the town square speaking to another woman would flit through then in through her mind, like the brightly colored lizards she sometimes noticed from her apartment window. She let the thought remain. Sure, she could walk a few blocks to the square and spy on him. But then what? What could she do after all?

Beyle's money supply was nearing its end. She now had to shop more carefully just before the market closed, when the vendors were more eager for a sale and the products were cheaper. Her meals became sparser, sometimes just beans and rice. Immanuel brought food from home at times. He never questioned her methods or her plans. They never discussed them at all.

Not that Beyle had plans anymore. She couldn't quite pinpoint when her drive to plan had vanished or if it had slowly melted away in the sun. She tried to recall that earlier organized self but found she could only make out its haziest outlines. And then those too proved undetectable. She drifted slowly through her days, buoyed only by the nighttime visits of Immanuel, whose ardor and expertise remained undiminished. Sometimes, she devoured the food Immanuel brought her; at other times, she stared at it blankly, uncomprehendingly. Sometimes, she imagined that Freydl or Dov-Ber would come to rescue her from this dusty paradise. She dreamed that she would awaken in her apartment back home and look out at the rain descending plentifully on the red leaves of the autumn trees lining her block. Sometimes, she dreamed that she was at Freydl's apartment, that they were sharing a Shabbas meal together, with wine, hallah, gefilte fish, matzoh ball soup, and roasted chicken that she had cooked, with minor variations, every week for years before the divorce. She would give Freydl the chicken leg as she preferred.

A rather burly man knocked on her door one day, interrupting her trance. He made sweeping gestures towards her and the studio apartment. Beyle had struggled without success to master the local language. But she understood that her days in the studio were limited. The burly man tacked a notice to the door and left. Beyle looked around in her cupboard, foraging for food. But the cupboard was bare. When had she last eaten?

A light touch on her shoulder from Immanuel awakened her. He carried her, now little more than skin and bones (no need to diet now!) to a wagon linked to a dirty white/gray mule. Instead of seating her in the wagon front seat, Immanuel placed her on a bed of straw in the wagon itself. Beyle felt the wagon lurch before she heard the rattling of the wheels and the clip-clop of the mule's hooves on the cobblestones.

She wondered where Immanuel was taking her, where she would presumably face some radical transition, perhaps, even her end. To meet Immanuel's family? Unlikely. The poorhouse? Were foreigners permitted there? Was she finally a tourist no more? Surely, not the workhouse. Even in her current state, even with her improved culinary skills, Beyle knew she wouldn't be of much use there. Potter's field? Was she still alive? She touched her hand on her heart, felt her pulse to be sure. Yes, yes, she was.

Her eyes wide to the heavens, Beyle saw the tops of buildings and trees drift by overhead. The light was at its brightest now. Surely nothing terrible could happen to her in broad daylight, out in the open. Or was the light in her mind? Surely Immanuel would not let anything happen to her. She never wanted to ask many questions about him; she didn't want to be too inquisitive or nosy. She didn't want to break the magic of their connection with the commonplace. She wanted them and their love to exist outside the sphere of negotiation and barter. And they had. They had succeeded. Still, she wished she knew Immanuel better. She wished she found a way to know him better. What did she really know of Immanuel? If Freydl had stayed, Beyle would've learned more without having to ask.

The wagon came to a sudden halt. Immanuel appeared over her and placed flowers all around her. She saw that they were flowers from the market and the fields, ordinary flowers, not like the ones he sold from carefully cultivated flower farms for the romantic couples on the square. She was pleased by their wildness, their unexpected shapes. She felt encased by red and violet and pink and orange. Was there yellow too? She looked around but didn't see any. Perhaps it was just above her head. She didn't have strength to look for it, even though she sensed its importance. Yellow would have brightened this pilgrimage. Yellow would have completed her.

Then Beyle thought of the white roses she purchased from Immanuel on the night they met. Why didn't she save them? She could have dried them out and pressed them in the pages of her guidebook. They might have served as a souvenir of that meeting and an anchor in the months that followed. Their presence might have enabled a different turn of events. Who knew? But Beyle tossed them in the trash bin, and the cleaning staff had removed them. Or at least, she must have. She had no memory of discarding them. Despite their clarity, the white roses, like her planned life, were now all in the distance, in the fog that threatened just behind the sunlight's brightness.

Beyle felt Freydl return to her. She felt her love for Immanuel reach its climax. In a bed of hay, surrounded by flowers, on a wagon moving to whereabouts unknown, Beyle felt Immanuel's love, not in its acrobatic agility, but as a force field of magnetic density, enveloping her finally, fully in its blackness.

"Phoenix, With Hat"

The house loomed before Khane as she trudged towards it, her suitcase-on-wheels rolling noisily behind her. It evoked for her the haunted houses on the lurid covers of the novels displayed in pharmacies and dime stores. There were too many balconies, cupolas, and gingerbread accessories, some of them jutting forth at strange angles and for no apparent visual reason. Still, although the house was painted in particularly gloomy tones of red and gray, Khane noted that the paint had been freshly applied and the grounds were carefully groomed. If the house didn't exude warmth, it certainly seemed neat and respectable.

Khane knew she couldn't be choosy. She needed a place where she could live, if not privately, then at least away from prying eyes. She'd heard that the rooming house run by a Madame Maisie would offer just such lodgings. To be sure, the Madame was known to be a bit nosy at first but would gradually adjust her level of nosiness to match the responses of the lodger. If the latter proved unforthcoming, she would withdraw. From everything she'd heard about Madame Maisie, and admittedly it hadn't been that much, Khane was confident she could interact comfortably with her. About her lodgers, Khane would have to wait and see … if she got that far.

As she walked up the path, Khane saw the curtains in one of the front windows move ever so slightly. Presumably the Madame was watching from inside. That was fine with Khane; a vigilant proprietress of a rooming house was an asset. Even before she could press the doorbell, the front door swung open, and Madame Maisie appeared before her. She was a tall woman in a mousy gray sweater over a brown cotton dress, her steel gray hair in a neatly upswept do and held in place by several rhinestone combs. Her smile seemed equally tidily arranged to Khane, and her hand was extended for a handshake.

Madame Maisie motioned for Khane to enter the house and follow her into the parlor, which appeared rarely (if ever) used. Without offering Khane a seat, Madame Maisie launched into an explanation of the honorific before her name something about her having mastered French in finishing school years ago. Khane was surprised she'd kept the name since that same honorific was often used, at least in an English-speaking context, to mean someone running a house of ill repute, which she knew Madame Maisie was not. Or was that only "Madam" without an "e" at the end? Khane wasn't sure. She would need to look up the difference between "Madame" and "Madam" in a dictionary some time. After Khane introduced herself as "Hannah Leventhal", she noted Madame Maisie's already cold smile grow a tad frostier yet. 'Hmm … '

Madame Maisie then proceeded to express her surprise that Khane brought her luggage to the first interview since she'd made it so clear on her promotional leaflets that potential lodgers were not supposed to do so. Khane hadn't heard anything about not bringing luggage to the interview, but she doubted it would have made a difference she had. She saw no point in making a separate trip to fetch her luggage. If this place met her initial approval, she saw no reason to "think it over" or delay the inevitable. And she believed her person would make a sufficiently favorable first impression to win her residency. When Madame Maisie asked her how she'd heard of her rooming house, Khane replied that a colleague had told her about it.

Hoping to move the interview process along, Khane let Madame Maisie know she was welcome to check on her references and that she would wait here in the meantime. As Madame Maisie left the room, Khane seated herself on a comfortable wing chair near the window. The pink sofa looked even less used than the chair and was probably a family heirloom of some sort. Khane observed that Madame Maisie noticed that she sat down without being granted permission to do so. She probably should have waited until Madame Maisie had left the room before seating herself but she was tired and perhaps not thinking entirely clearly. Such errors could determine whether she was accepted into the rooming house. She was pleased she was wearing her violet suit, which flattered her figure and lent her an air of elegance, and her hat with a half-veil. She only wore them on special occasions, which this certainly was.

As Khane waited in the parlor for Madame Maisie's return, she hoped that her references would be positive. She had no reason to suspect they wouldn't be but still one never knew. Khane was grateful for her job at the old age home and felt she did her utmost there to perform with professionalism and collegiality. She quickly memorized the names of all the residents in her wing and became acquainted with their medical and personal histories. Khane brought them food in the dining hall and all of their basic needs were met. At night, she made sure they were comfortable in bed and had taken their medications. If one of them had an accident in a private room or in a communal area, Khane was the first to clean it up. Her many years of working in her parents' general store had ingrained in her the habits and importance of customer service. The elderly had more specific needs but in the end were not so very different from the store customers. They too expected to be waited on and have their needs met with a pleasant demeanor.

Madame Maisie seemed quite pleased with Khane's supervisor Mr. Van Kirk's reference, even as she was surprised that Khane was sitting exactly as she had left her. She granted Khane admission to the rooming house, stating briefly the house rules such as no males permitted on the premises, only week notice was required to vacate the premises, and rent was due every Friday by noon. All of these seemed reasonable to Khane, and she readily agreed and followed Madame Maisie up the stairs and down a long carpeted corridor to her room.

The fussiness that characterized the house's exterior and downstairs was largely absent in the room itself. She had expected to see the room choked by flowered pink wallpaper, but was pleased by the solid wash of subdued colors of grays and dark purples. The room was furnished with end tables, a comfortable chair, and a writing desk. Madame Maisie informed her that the corridor was furnished with two washrooms, one at either end. Although Khane was disappointed that the washroom wasn't connected to the bedroom itself, she nodded her head. When Madame Maisie closed the door behind her, Khane removed her hat and sat gratefully down in the chair.

***

At dinner that evening, Khane met the two other lodgers, Stella Norcliffe and Agnes Robertson. Miss Norcliffe was a stage actress, and Miss Robertson was a typist who also had some receptionist duties. The custom of the house was for all lodgers to be addressed by "Miss" followed by their family name and not by their first names. Khane heard Madame Maisie catch herself before almost saying "Christian" instead of "first" names. Khane wondered about her own admission into the home. Had she truly impressed the Madame? Or was the Madame feeling a financial pinch, having two rooms available to let? Giving a false name was never even considered. Khane's parents had taught her to be proud of her heritage. Besides, there were too many official records, including her place of employment, which had her real name. It was enough that she used the Anglicized form of her first name rather than the "Khane" with which she was called by her parents. Khane knew better than to tell Madame Maisie that she knew Eunice, the Madame's cook and housekeeper well. Quite well, in fact.

As Miss Norcliffe and Miss Robertson shared information about their backgrounds that evening (and on subsequent ones), Khane remained quiet. Miss Norcliffe's parents were mortified by her career choice. Although Miss Robertson's parents were pleased with her having steady work, they wanted her to settle down. Khane judged Miss Robertson to be close to forty, a good ten years older than herself, and wondered if Miss Robertson's idea of settling down was different than her parents'. She appeared to be thoroughly content to reside in Madame Maisie's rooming house.

'What about you, Miss Leventhal? Tell us about yourself. Where are you from?'

Listening to the easy chatter of the lodgers, Khane was jolted out a reverie that required a listening focus and an absenting of self by the questions posed by Miss Robertson. The room grew quiet as all heads turned to Khane.

'I grew up in a small town. A very quiet life really. Not much to tell.'

Khane looked down into her potato leek soup, hoping that her drab response managed to deflect the curiosity of the other lodgers and Madame Maisie. Had Miss Robertson just been making conversation or was she, in particular, interested in learning more about Khane? Perhaps it really is just nerves, Khane assured herself. Fortunately, Eunice entered the room at that moment to bring in the main course of salmon and asparagus and to clear away the soup dishes. Khane murmured, 'Thank you' and complimented her on the meal. Eunice had cautioned her not to do so but she just couldn't oblige. Eunice's cooking was so tasty she couldn't help herself. Far more skilled than Mame's cooking, Khane realized somewhat guiltily (blasphemously?) when she first tasted it. No one, including Madame Maisie, commented on Khane's unwillingness to share her story or her courtesy to Eunice.

***

Of course, if they knew her story, Khane thought one night when the questioning had bordering on grilling (Won't you tell us just one thing, dear Miss Leventhal?), she wouldn't be in this house. And there weren't many places for her to go. She needed to be here.

She wondered most nights upstairs in her room how her parents were managing. Aside from public school and Main Street, her parents' store and the apartment above it had been Khane's world for all of her life. Khane had assumed she would end her days there. She thought of its dimness and the long aisles filled with all sorts of goods. The store seemed to have everything, and people came from miles around to shop there. As a little girl, Khane's favorite aisle was the candy aisle. She loved the Mary Janes, the licorice, the nougats, and the rock candy. By the register in the front were the especially appealing canes – peppermint, watermelon, and sour cherry – housed in round transparent jars with lids and arranged in tiers to entice children waiting in the checkout line, sometimes alone, or rather more often, with their parents.

When she was a very little girl, Khane was sometimes permitted a sweet when she'd done particularly well in her religious studies. Tate, her father, would say, 'Go ahead, Khanele. But just one.' He didn't want learning to be connected with bodily pleasures in her mind as he repeatedly told her, but, buoyed by her scholastic excellence, couldn't help but relent to her entreaties. For her part, Khane loved the sweetness of the candy dissolving in her mouth. Sometimes she wondered if what she loved most at such moments was being called "Khanele" by her father. In the diminutive form of her name she heard his despair momentarily lifted.

Khane studied with Tate in the back room of the store in what amounted to a study. The room was dominated by Tate's enormous desk and bookcases rising from floor to ceiling lined with sacred texts. There were volumes on ethics, law, and mysticism and numerous volumes of the Bibles and Talmud, along with their commentaries from across the centuries. There were books lying flat on the books in the bookcase; there were books piled high on the desk and on chairs. Of course, no sacred text was permitted on the floor or Khane was certain there would have been books there, too. What he lacked in business sense Tate more than compensated for in teaching skills. He was a patient and imaginative teacher able to draw his pupil into far-reaching reflection. And under his tutelage, Khane blossomed as a pupil. They were often so engrossed in their study that Mame had to knock on the door to let them know supper was ready upstairs.

Of course, Khane's parents wanted her to attend a religious school where she could receive all-day instruction and interact with girls of her age and be a part of an educational institution. But in this small town that was impossible. Such a school didn't exist; there weren't even enough people to support a synagogue. Tate regularly lamented having to pray alone in his study, uncertain of the trajectory of his prayers expressed without a quorum. In fact, for most of her life, Khane's family was the only one in town of their background. And so Khane went to public school where she excelled and won academic prizes. Although she had friends at school, Khane was not permitted to go to their homes and was discouraged from bringing them to the small apartment over the store. Khane wasn't explicitly discouraged, to be sure, but somehow it was conveyed to her that visitors from school would not be appropriate. Khane understood public school as utterly separate – a realm apart – from home. Her few school friends understood and never pressed the matter.

Although her teachers had hoped she would pursue her studies in college, Khane was needed by her parents in the store. Tate-Mame were grateful to the townsfolk for their acceptance and support, and the customers moved freely and politely among them. And yet there was always a barrier between Khane and her parents on the one hand and the customers and other representatives of the outside world on the other. This was how it was, and always would be, Khane assumed, whenever she thought about it, which really wasn't very often at all.

Eunice was the one exception. Khane befriended Eunice only after her formal schooling ended, although she'd been coming to the store for years. Eunice's mother sent her at least once a week for the groceries. Their friendship began with a hat. When Eunice came to the register one day to pay for her items, Khane noticed her hat, a dramatic number with a brim extending low on one side and an oversized bow on the top opposite side and complimented her on it.

'That is a grand hat!'

'Thank you. I made it myself. I'll make one for you, Eunice responded,' smiling widely.

'I don't think my parents would let me wear a hat like that.'

Eunice shrugged at this response and explained to Khane how the hat was constructed and the materials needed to construct it. No one was in the store at that moment, and the two proceeded to talk at length about clothes and fabrics. Khane's mother had taught her to sew but she'd never made hats yet. She hadn't even considered making them.

'They're not expensive. I make them from scraps of fabric I pick up here and there. My aunt or ladies in the neighborhood give me scraps, too,' Eunice said.

Several days later, a box without a return address arrived in the mail. When she opened it, there was a hat, similar to the one that Khane had admired, but with a polka-dotted half-veil attached to it. Inside the hat was a carefully handwritten note that said: 'I think you will look good in this. Eunice.' When Khane next saw Eunice in the store, she thanked her and, without further consideration, invited her to a walk in the park later that week. The two had been friends ever since.

***

Eunice's cooking skills were every bit as advanced as her sewing ones. And these were on display in Madame Maisie's rooming house. She was trained by her mother and then by a distant relative named Bertha, who worked for many years in the rooming house, even before it was a rooming house. Khane marveled at the hearty goodness of the yams, the green beans sometimes made with almond slivers, sometimes with garlic, the roast chicken always golden and tender. All of Eunice's dishes were kept in the oven or on the stove for just the right amount of time and seasoned vividly with spices Khane could never identify. And here, in the rooming house, she didn't dare ask Eunice. Khane felt that she was already testing social propriety by her unflagging compliments and unfailingly polite greetings. And yet perhaps she wasn't. Khane wasn't always sure what was socially acceptable where standard politeness ended and genial social interaction began.

Sometimes, upstairs in her rooming house room after dinner, reading the Torah with its commentaries as she'd done with Tate, Khane considered trying to catch Eunice's eye after dinner or slip into the kitchen, however briefly. Only she never did. She needed to stay in the rooming house just a bit longer. Perhaps someday soon, when she felt more established, they could take walks in the park or in the woods, although they might be more conspicuous among the trees if they were found. Perhaps. Khane always aimed to study several verses, sometimes a chapter, of the Torah before going to sleep. For that one routine in her life now so thoroughly altered, Tate would have been pleased.

***

That day was indistinguishable from any other. There was a cool breeze in the morning, and the fragrance of flowers and freshly mowed grass in the air. Khane performed the inventory of stock, walking briefly up and down the aisles, noting that they were low on whole-wheat flour and pickles. She checked the books and saw again how many accounts were still outstanding. Tate could never refuse a poor customer who needed credit, despite Mame's insistence that they weren't running a charity. Khane smiled that day, for in some measure, they actually were, even it wasn't called that.

He appeared suddenly behind her as she was bending to straighten some stock on the shelves. The canned and preserved goods aisle, in fact. Feeling something cold pressed against her temple, Khane heard the words:

'Go to the front door, lock it, and put the closed sign on the door. Don't make a sound. Do as I tell you. You're not better than us now, uppity kike bitch.'

As she moved to carry out his command, Khane tried frantically to think of an escape route. But he was right behind her. The gloom of the store served his purposes; no one would see inside or think anything of it. After she had done as told, the man gestured for her to go into the back office. There, he bent Khane over her father's desk, the tractate *Kidushin* opened ironically before her. Now she would never have to be concerned with the terms of betrothal contracts, she thought. He lifted her dress and slip, yanked down her bloomers, and performed his ruination. His hand covered her mouth, and his gun never left her temple. Although it felt like an eternity, Khane had no idea how much time had passed. A few minutes? Fifteen? As it went on and on, she drifted outside her body, not looking down at herself, but away, into the very depths of the jams and jellies. She really would have to check their expiration dates, especially the blackberry ones. And then thinking of depths, the passage from the Psalms *Shir ha-maalot mi-maamakim keratikha Adonai* flitted through her mind. Never in her brief life had she had to call upon those words.

He left as suddenly as he appeared. The words he addressed to her in the canned goods aisle were the only ones he ever uttered to Khane. Her parents were both upstairs the entire time. After all of their warnings about avoiding certain parts of town or even side streets and never walking outside unaccompanied at all after dark, it had happened here, under their very noses. Her mother was probably cleaning or preparing supper or darning her father's socks. Her father was certain to be at the balm that was his sacred texts, relieved to be released, however briefly, from the store that was his livelihood and prison.

Khane straightened her clothes and hair and reopened the store. She tossed her bloodied bloomers into the basement furnace fire that night after her parents went to bed. Her gray work dress, adorned only by a scalloped black collar, she hung in a corner of her closet. Mame, who had sewn it for her and to her specifications (no flower prints please!!), would inquire after it if it went missing or if Khane didn't wear it again. Bitterly, Khane noted how the dress wasn't even torn or damaged in any way. She couldn't bring herself to look at the clock.

***

Khane didn't intend to tell Tate-Mame or anyone else what befell her, or how she was felled, she thought sometimes. She continued to work in the store, as she'd always done, rising early, returning upstairs just before dinner. Yet one day, a week after "the event", Khane couldn't get out of bed. Growing up in the shadow-filled store, apart from the townspeople, Khane had never expected happiness to be her birthright. But nothing had prepared her for this. The blackness that enveloped her was a heavy, animated monster from which she couldn't seem to escape. She couldn't make herself rise and see her devastation moving about in the world as if it could be accommodated there. She simply lacked the strength to lift her body upright.

Her parents were uneasy, having never seen her confined to the bed in this way. Mame regularly felt her forehead and took her temperature. They brought her meals and seltzer water. Mame sat with her on her narrow bed and recited Psalms to her. Sometimes, she would stop and ask Khane what was wrong. Tate came upstairs throughout the day, sometimes with Mame, often alone.

After Khane had been in bed for nearly a week, Mame said she was going to call the doctor. Khane fell into a panic at this announcement. She dropped to her knees, pleading with Mame not to do that. When she'd finally extracted a promise from Mame that she wouldn't, Khane returned in bed to relief. The mention of the doctor had somehow penetrated her despair. She'd have to rise now and re-enter the world.

That re-entry was halting. Her parents found her at once slow and skittish. Khane was now afraid to be left alone in the store. She couldn't concentrate on the accounts and occasionally misplaced items on the shelves. Mame would discover fresh produce in the canned goods in the paper section or potatoes with the ketchup and condiments. Not even close. Only at the cash register was Khane able to interact with the customers with her usual courtesy and efficiency.

When Khane missed her period, she realized she'd have to tell someone. When Eunice was next in the store, they made plans to take one of their walks in the park. Khane didn't quite know what to do in the meantime. The days until their meeting seemed to drag interminably. Sometimes she would stare off into space, gazing blankly and unseeing at the portraits of the ancestors from the Old Country on the living room wall or through the window at the hazy streetscape. Her mother would come upon her in this way and shudder in fear. She'd put a shawl around Khane and tell her when it was time for a meal or to go to bed.

Up until the very moment that Khane told Eunice what had happened to her, she wasn't sure she'd have the courage to go forward with the revelation. But she did, somehow. Eunice remained silent for nearly a minute. Perhaps because of Eunice's silence, Khane found herself able to think and speak with deliberation.

'I'm going to keep the baby. Not because I want it. I don't. It's going to devastate my parents. But I've heard about the home measures, and I'm not going to throw myself down the stairs or stick a knitting needle into my uterus or douche with turpentine or lye or visit a witch doctor in a back alley. My life, even after this, still matters. It has to.'

Khane wasn't sure where these words came from. They sounded more like a speech than something she'd tell a friend. But having said them, she was glad for the speaking, for their utterance. Making sure that no one saw them, Eunice hugged Khane briefly but intensely. She said she knew somewhere she could go, a place where she could stay to have the baby. She said she'd look into it and let Khane know very soon.

Something about Eunice's "very soon" jolted Khane into the realization that she couldn't delay telling her parents much longer. The fog in which she'd been living hadn't lifted but she'd have to find a way through it. She wondered how Tate-Mame would manage the store without her, not that she'd been of very much use lately. Would they disown her? Would they tear their clothes in mourning? Would Mame burst into tears? Would Tate stop speaking to her? Would Tate-Mame disown her? She would wait until she heard back from Eunice before telling them.

Eunice came by the store the next day and told Khane, 'Everything's arranged. As soon as you start to show, you should go to the "place". I'll take you there. They're expecting you. They're asking for a little money for room and board. But if you can't pay, they won't turn you away.'

About six weeks later, Khane felt the time had come. Her clothes had begun to tighten ever so slightly. She let Eunice know she would be ready to be driven to "the place" the next day. That evening, Khane asked Tate-Mame to remain at the table after supper. She repeated step-by-step the events of that day in the store, omitting only the words spoken by the man, feeling strangely disassociated from the narrative, as if she were recounting all of this from afar, as if she had been asked to relay the unfortunate circumstances of a friend. She wondered briefly in the telling if "misfortunestance" was a word. Khane told Tate-Mame she would be leaving home tomorrow to have the child that would be born of the event.

Her parents were silent during and after what now, twice recounted, felt like a recitation, a dirge. Like Eunice, they couldn't seem to find their way to words. Her father's hands started to tremble. Her mother stood up and started to scour the kitchen sink. What Khane most feared did not occur. There was no weeping or rending of clothing; no shouts or threats of being disowned. If only there had been. Instead, there was an anguish that seeped soundlessly into everything – the worn objects of furniture, the walls of the apartment, into the clothes and very bodies of Tate-Mame. When she went to bed that night, she didn't hear them murmuring to each other as they usually did. She listened for that and for muffled weeping. But there was nothing. Only silence.

All that night Khane lay in bed rigid without sleep. Memories flooded back to her. Mame on a rare break from the store beaming with pride at the back of the school auditorium when Khane received an award for scholastic achievement in English. Baking challah for the Sabbath with Mame, feeling Mame's arms guiding her through the kneading process. Mame's sigh followed by clucking as she reviewed the store's green leather, gilded ledger. How strange that such an elegant book contained such grim tidings, Khane thought. Tate's hand lightly touching Mame's shoulder as she stared down at the closed ledger, as if he were begging for her forgiveness, as if steeling her to face the uncertain future, as if thanking her for being there. What gnarled intimacy born of a financial ledger documenting a doggedly determined but barely breathing enterprise! The unassuming appeal of the meals the three of them shared on the Sabbath itself. The burden somchow lifted from Tate-Mame's faces and bodies as they savored the onset of their brief liberation from the burdens of the store. The fluttering of the flowered ivory lace curtains in her bedroom window as the family rested on Sabbath afternoon, as she drifted from melody into slumber and then back. These elders, this store, these spartan rooms above it this had been Khane's world and here she had always expected to spend and end the days granted to her. Who would she be without them? Without all this that had been hers? How would she be when cut off from it – a woman truncated, a daughter asunder? Hadn't she been content, in the end (and this was an end, of sorts)? Why did she tell Tate-Mame what happened to her? And what words did she use to tell? Could she have found others? Wouldn't it have been far better to slip away into the night rather than bring such … ?

And then this choice quagmire: was the shattering (and impending loss) of the bulwark that Tate-Mame and she constructed against a world variously polite, indifferent, hostile, welcoming, not "other" exactly but always just outside their own sheer curtain more terrible than the horror she had endured during those fated minutes? Khane continued to replay the images, both still and moving, and to pose and reframe these questions until dawn broke through the tightly drawn curtains and her own disquiet.

***

The "place" to which Eunice brought her, following an early morning departure and a three-hour journey, was a shack in the country occupied by a woman named Althea. Eunice hugged Khane at the fork in the road that led to the woman's shack since Althea had asked that Eunice not bring Khane herself to the front door. Just before she left, Eunice gave Khane a list of chores conveyed to her by Althea, most of which seemed light, including cleaning and preparing the food for dinner. Khane wondered why Althea didn't give Khane the list of chores directly but decided not to ask.

'You take care, hear? I'll come get you soon enough.'

Khane nodded, and the two women hugged. She stood to watch Eunice drive away in a cousin's run-down pickup truck.

Althea and Khane created a routine without ever naming it as such. Khane performed the housework, which left Althea time and energy to do the laundry and darning she took in to make extra money. Every week, she gave Althea money from the funds Mame had given her the morning she left the apartment above the store. Mame had insisted that she take it. Sometimes, at night, Khane would read to Althea from the Torah in the original Hebrew and then translate for her. Althea loved to hear the sounds of the Hebrew. She said she felt she could hear God in the sounds, as if He weren't behind a screen anymore. Khane, who'd never before shared her bedroom (let alone her bed), slept on a cot only a few yards from Althea. When she woke up in the middle of the night with a start, wondering where she was. Althea's steady breathing reminded and then grounded her.

Sometimes, Khane took a barefoot late-night walk in a nearby thicket. The calls of the wildlife, if not directed at her, seemed to include her, to draw her in. The stars winked at her in embrace. Despite the heaviness and swollenness of her body, she felt a lightness she hadn't felt in years. She ran from the thicket into the fallow field nearby, the tall grasses parting for her, their near-roots wet and soothing against her feet until she arrived, utterly spent, at Althea's rickety doorstep. She felt that between those trees and in those fields, in the inchoate, roiling exhilaration found there, she was where she was meant to be, where she was most herself. Not a loving and dutiful daughter in a general store and the apartment above it, schooled in the sacred texts and the ways of the sages by a scholar storekeeper father and an equally devout (if less learned) mother, and not a wild woman at all, but a woman of the wild, outside the bounds of civilization altogether, a woman whose meaning was best conferred by bare feet on green, whose next steps would be gathering berries and nuts and other edibles tucked away far from the central path, and finding dreamless slumber beneath stars and amongst other creatures who rejected the threshold of human existence. The words of the High Holidays prayer "*U-netaneh tokef*" "*Adam yesodo me-afar ve-sofo le-afar*" reverberated often through her mind as neon billboards. Yes, from dust are we forged and to dust shall we finally return, but what of this dust in between? But as she inhaled the scents of the earth, she knew it wasn't dust that was calling to her, but *adamah, arets* soil, ground, in all of its generosity. In all of its unity, despite its specificity and variety. And in all of its unknowable vastness – the earth itself.

Closing the door softly behind her, Khane would invariably hear Althea sleepily call out, 'That you, doll baby?'

'Yes, it's me. It's Khane,' she'd respond. "Your doll, with baby" was what she really wanted to answer but never did. Still, it was their own private call-and-response.

Throughout those weeks, working with Althea or at rest, Khane thought often about Tate-Mame. How were they getting on in her absence? In her gone-ness? She thought about the spaces of the apartment and the store, the familiar figures inside them, and her own self no longer in physical proximity, or even relation, to them. The touch of her father's hands on her head – the only sanctioned occasion for his touch now that she was an adult – as he blessed her before Yom Kippur suddenly came to her. She'd always felt such joy afterwards, that with his blessing graced by his touch, she could face whatever difficulties would arise on the fast day and the year to come. But now she wondered who was doing the sweeping and dusting, especially in the far-away corners and crevices were getting done. Mame, with her arthritis, and Tate, with his bad back, couldn't reach that far. And they couldn't really afford to hire anyone.

And she had so many questions to ask Tate-Mame about their lives before her – questions she always assumed could ask later. Only she wouldn't see them later. Now there was no later. What was their life like in the Old Country? How did they make the voyage over? How did they come to settle upon the town? True, she knew it wouldn't have been easy to elicit this information, as Tate-Mame made it clear that they had no wish to speak about the past. Such inquiries had only led to deflections or changing the topic. But Khane could have persisted, could have found an artful way forward. Of that she was sure.

And Khane wondered how Tate-Mame would have responded if she tried to remain at home. But she couldn't ask it of them; she couldn't risk the answer. She couldn't bear for her parents to see her in this way. Away from the store and the apartment, Khane realized again she'd always envisioned herself remaining in the store, helping and then eventually caring for her parents when needed and then keeping the store going as a memorial to them. Once or twice (perhaps more), she'd allowed herself the fantasies of marriage and/or teaching school – passing on what Tate-Mame had taught her to her children or students. But then she banished them from her mind and body, brushing her skirt or straightening her collar in the process. In any case, those fantasies seemed thoroughly out of the question now.

When Khane's contractions began in earnest, Eunice was sent word through Althea's grapevine. Althea felt she needed an extra pair of hands to help her. But the birth process went smoothly; the baby was born before she arrived. The baby's vigorous cries greeted Eunice as she entered the shack. While Althea slept on her cot, Khane stayed up all night to hold her daughter rocking her to sleep and feeding her. If tradition permitted a child to be named after the living, she would've named her "Eunice". Instead, she named her Dinah.

***

One night, several months into her stay at Madame Maisie's rooming house, Khane felt it was safe to make contact with Eunice. It was a rare evening when Madame Maisie hadn't joined them for dinner. Miss Norcliffe and Miss Robertson had gone out for a constitutional, as they sometimes did. Khane was glad that Miss Robertson had finally stopped inviting her to join them on the constitutionals. She slipped into the kitchen and gave Eunice a quick embrace before she could protest.

'You could go on any evening but Thursdays are best.'

'Please let them know I'll be ready this Thursday. Two days from today. Thank you, Eunice.'

Khane waited a half-hour in her room until she heard Madame close the door to her room. Then she tiptoed down the stairs and out of the rooming house. She was careful to follow the directions Eunice gave her. Khane felt strangely protected here, not as if she belonged in this neighborhood, but as if Eunice's hand was extended to support her.

The door opened after three knocks in quick succession. The woman introduced herself as Louella, a deacon at Eunice's church. She said Dinah was doing just fine and lifted her from the cradle and into her mother's outstretched arms. Khane played with Dinah for over an hour. Dinah seemed to respond to Khane's cooing and other mother-baby happy noises. Dinah stared right back at her, offering what Khane was sure was the outline of a smile. She wished she could stay longer. Khane wished she could stay up with her as she had done on the night Dinah was born. But she had to return. Khane left the agreed-upon amount of funds on the front table, bade Louella a good night, and left. She knew that Dinah was being well cared for, even if that care was being given in a home outside her tradition, and that she, Khane, would manage in this world, this very different world.

The days at the old age home were uneventful but fulfilling. Khane's contentment with her employment remained. The professionalism that had so impressed Mr. Van Kirk at her initial interview continued to this day. Mr. Van Kirk never mentioned having spoken with Madame Maisie or her new place of residence. Khane realized Mr. Van Kirk never questioned the address Khane had given on her initial application form, although she'd written down Althea's remote address, thinking it was safer than using Eunice's address. He might have wondered but needed her contributions just as much Madame Maisie did. Not for the first time did Khane reflect on the recent twists of good fortune brought about by the love of her friend Eunice and the needs of others: the old age home, Louella, and Madame Maisie.

One night, while walking to Louella's, Khane heard footsteps behind her. She decided to stop. When she stopped, the footsteps did, as well. She accelerated her pace, but the footsteps didn't flag. At first, she wondered if Miss Norcliffe or Miss Robertson were following her. But some heaviness, some effort in the tread, told her otherwise. She realized Madame Maisie was following her. When she opened the door and saw Dinah in Louella's arms, she forgot the Madame. She couldn't take her eyes from the child born to her of brutality. She laughed at the gurgling; she felt Dinah's fingers tighten around her hand. She talked with Louella about Dinah's bowel movements, her eating habits, and her every burp, cough, and sneeze.

Khane stayed with Louella late that night, not knowing what fate awaited her at the rooming house. She fell asleep in the worn wing chair in Louella's front room. Louella draped an afghan over her as she drifted into sleep, overcome by the drama of Madame Maisie following her and the joy of spending time with her daughter.

The next morning, Khane kissed and caressed Dinah and embraced Louella upon leaving, repeating her appreciation, as she did when she left at night. As she returned to Madame Maisie's rooming house, Khane wondered if her time there was over, if all the plans carefully devised with Eunice had come to naught. She wondered if she'd willfully brought this downfall upon herself, just as she'd wondered if she were to blame for the event in the store. Would she be expelled from the house? From the town itself? Would Eunice be let go? Why hadn't she been warmer to Madame Maisie? Why hadn't she spent more time with her as did the Misses Norcliffe and Robertson? Why had she rebuffed the overtures of Miss Robertson who could have put in a good word on her behalf?

On this walk back to Madame Maisie's rooming house, Khane thought of the hat gifted her by Eunice so many years ago. Admittedly out of fashion now, but still stylish in its way. She thought of Eunice who had crafted it so lovingly and who had saved her from so much tribulation and distress. She thought of their walks together because they couldn't really be together in either of their homes or in public dining spaces. She thought of their laughter, their pleasure in each other's company, in their bodies so close, sometimes brushing, in their bond unshakeable, despite the odds. She saw Eunice's graceful neck rising from the collar of her Sunday-best cream collared dress, of her way of looking at Khane, of seeing her as she was before her. She thought of Eunice's work-hands, work-worn yet still silky, that Khane would clasp when the rare opportunity would reveal itself. Was it just the lotion that Eunice used? Khane felt a smile begin to form, knowing that it had more to do with the mystery of hands, the alchemy of touch. Eunice's touch, their together-touch. And she felt now the euphoria that reverberated throughout her body when Eunice did not withdraw and even returned, or exceeded in strength, Khane's clasp.

If her belongings weren't on the floor in a pile in Madame Maisie's rooming house vestibule, Khane would go up to her room and don her hat from Eunice. She'd figure something out. Eunice would. She wouldn't let Eunice go. She wouldn't let Dinah go. Together, they would find a way. Her family now. In the front and the now. In the front of the now.

II. Sons

"Called Away in the Spirit"

Silas didn't run away from home, not exactly. For one thing, he was twenty-three years old, an adult. And for another, because of legal and societal standards. He had his birth certificate, social security card, driver's license, and voter registration card as proof if he were questioned. The few times he'd gone to bars, Silas was carded and given the once-over and sometimes more, even after his ID had been inspected. Maybe it was because of his baby face – still only the slightest trace of facial hair above his mouth – and slightness of build. Silas hadn't voted yet here, but he would, he promised himself, once he was settled down in wherever it was he was headed. For another, he told his grandmother up front that it was time for him to go, that he was leaving. His grandmother looked up from her knitting, which she said kept her eyes strong, and said, 'Let me pack you something to eat.' That was Gran – no attempts to stop him or persuade him to stay, no questions about where he was going or the plans he'd made. What and when he wanted to tell her, he would, that was what Gran believed.

She was knitting a scarf, of gray, with flecks of rust and black, when Silas told her about his decision. Gran liked to mix colors, some unusual, others not. She said it kept things interesting. And it also depended on whom Gran was knitting for. Gran gave her knitwear away as gifts or for charity and sometimes sold it. Some of Gran's clients liked to be surprised by her color combinations, such as teal and purple or ginger and Kelly green. Gran had given a sweater with that color combination to Maggie Smithers, a neighbor down the road. Maggie wore it proudly to church socials and praised Gran in front of the other parishioners much to Gran's embarrassment.

But Gran was pleased, too. Silas could see that. These were colors you wouldn't think would work but did because Gran knew how to make them come together.

She did a lot of different things to make ends meet, did his Gran. She cleaned houses, baked cakes, cobbler, and pies, did sewing of all kinds, and not just darning and mending, but new dresses, skirts, blouses, and such. Gran had orders from out of state for her pecan pie, and her peach cobbler won first prize two years in a row at the state fair. Gran approached her baked goods with the same eclectic methods as her knitting. Folks would always try to figure out the exact ingredients. Sometimes, Gran would share, sometimes she wouldn't. 'That's my secret recipe,' Gran would then say in response to the questioning, smiling to soften what she knew was seen as her abruptness of manner. It was all good-natured, but folks still wanted to know.

She put aside the scarf, stood up from the sofa, and walked into the kitchen without waiting for a response from Silas. What was there to say? Wherever he was going, he'd still need to eat. Standing in the doorway, Silas watched Gran move around the kitchen, efficiently extracting various items from the fridge. She'd be sure to pack some cold cuts, chicken, cole slaw, potato salad, and cookies. And greens, of course. Growing up, Gran always made sure Silas ate his greens and everything she placed on the table before him. And yet Silas was never obese. He supposed it was a combination of factors – the healthy food Gran prepared, his genetic predisposition (Gran was also slim), and all the exercise he got riding his bike and completing his chores around Gran's house and land. Gran never referred to her land as a farm. It was too small for that. And yet, with her cow, chickens, goats, apple trees and vegetable patches, Gran always had plenty for herself and Silas, and sometimes enough to sell on market day in town. When some of her friends saw Silas standing alongside Gran in church or at the market, they'd say to Gran, 'You need to fatten that boy up!' or 'He needs some meat on his bones!' But Gran just smiled and said, 'My boy eats just fine.' Silas felt himself blushing in response to such exchanges.

Silas stepped away from watching Gran packing food in the kitchen and headed up to his room. He was all packed:

underwear, jeans, t-shirts, sweaters, a few dress shirts and slacks, and toiletries. Both of his suitcases were nearly full. He'd pack Gran's food in his backpack, of course. Everyone on the bus would smell Gran's cooking; there'd be no way around that. Silas would be happy to share with other passengers if it came to that. That happened once before when he went with his classmates on an outing to a nearby nature preserve. A few of the other kids crowded around his lunch and asked him for some. And that was just when he'd had a sandwich and some side treats. As he'd grown older, Gran's packed meals had grown more elaborate, more enticing. There'd be casseroles and chicken pot pie and curries. He never told Gran he gave away some of his lunches, but he assumed she knew. The portions she packed were really too big for one boy to eat.

Silas brought the suitcases down to the front door, making separate trips for each and taking care not to scratch the wooden stairs with the wheels or the bottoms of the suitcases. This time, Silas hadn't followed Gran's regularly repeated advice to pack lightly. Seeing that Gran was still in the kitchen, he opened the front door and brought the suitcases out to her pick-up truck. He loaded them up carefully, not because there was anything breakable inside, but because he didn't want to pull a muscle right before leaving town. That would be ridiculous and just his luck, too! Well, once the food was here, he would be ready to go. The only thing missing from this scene was a loyal dog looking anxiously on. But Gran never allowed him a pet of any kind. 'Just another mouth to feed,' she responded to his repeated pleas.

Gran came outside, her hands full with the food she'd prepared. Silas didn't ask what was in the bags. As always, he'd get what Gran gave him. He managed to fit all of the bags in his backpack. Gran then gestured for him to get in the passenger seat, and she climbed in the driver's seat. Gran was a steady driver, much better than Silas was, in fact, with his tendency to drive slow and let others pass him on the road.

The evening sky, streaked with orange, pink, and purple, reminded Silas of one of Gran's most memorable scarves. Was that the one she'd given to Mrs. Johnson, the high school janitor's wife, after she had come back from the hospital from her first round of chemotherapy? Silas couldn't be sure and didn't want to ask and distract Gran from her driving. Her steady driving came at a price; conversation was never forthcoming when Gran was behind the wheel. Silas hoped Gran wouldn't drive by his high school, from which he'd only barely managed to graduate. Squeaked by, as they say.

Even with the chug-chug of the motor (or muffler?) of Gran's truck along the highway, the sounds of the country air were audible. The song of the crickets, the buzzing of mosquitoes and gnats, the barking of dogs. Somewhere, far away, a howling of some kind. Even having lived all his life in this country setting, there were still so many sounds unnamed to Silas.

When Gran drove down Main Street, the familiar landmarks came into view: the post office, the pharmacy, the late night diner sharper than ever, despite the deepening of evening. Silas was torn between looking over at Gran, sitting upright and staring at the road ahead in silence, and outside at the place he was leaving for the first time and possibly forever.

There was the ice cream parlor, where Silas got his first summer job. All of the ice cream was made by hand, and Silas knew himself to be getting strong that summer. Strong through ice cream! There had never been very exotic flavors there, as Silas had seen in other shops, despite the efforts of the owner's son to convince his father to branch out. Just the classic flavors such as mint chocolate chip, butter almond, pistachio, rocky road, coffee (not java or espresso), cinnamon, and of course, chocolate, strawberry, and vanilla. That summer, Silas learned the power of simple sweetness, of sustaining tradition when it came to treats. The parlor had round bistro tables and a marble counter, with a mirror behind it, in front of which lovebirds snuck glances at themselves over ice cream and between kisses. A green-and-white wide-striped awning fronted the window's exterior. Working in the parlor that summer cured him forever of a craving for ice cream. Since then, Silas associated ice cream with work, with serving and furthering the pleasure of strangers.

And there was the white-steepled church flashing by, on whose doorsteps his mother had deposited him when he was a small boy. 'Nothing will happen to you here. I just need to take care of something. I'll be back soon. Be a good boy,' his mother said to him fussing with his shirt collar. His mother had been especially fidgety, anxious to go but not to let him go. But then his mother was always anxious, and perhaps that day no more so than any other. That was what Silas most remembered about his mother: her anxiety and her nervousness. Sometimes, when her boyfriend at the time would come upon her unexpectedly, his mother would flinch. Silas assumed the boyfriend noticed her flinching. How could he not? But he never said anything, at least not in front of Silas. Sometimes, she would jump when she heard her boyfriend close the front door behind, the heavy tread following close behind.

Silas wandered into the chapel that day and sat on one of the long hard pews in the church, his legs not reaching the floor. At that time, Silas had only been to church a few times before – when their neighbors invited them for their son's baptism and once, unexpectedly, on Easter. Most of the time, he just watched the activity outside the church. He would sit on the curb across the street and watch as the worshippers arrived in their freshly pressed Sunday best. He especially admired the wide-brimmed hats shading the ladies' faces. Sometimes he made a point to watch the church after the services were over, noticing how the preacher would shake the hands of each soul as they left the service. That was what Gran called the folks in church – souls. He could see them complimenting him on his sermon, thanking him for the inspiration of his example and his words. The children never ran around or shouted as they did when school let out, although some occasionally tugged at their parents' hands or clothing when the conversation with the preacher or other souls grew too long. Silas admired the decorum, the sense of belonging and well being that characterized the gestures and framed the scene. He always stayed until the last parishioner departed, even as he tried not to attract attention himself.

After his mother deposited him in the chapel, the sun streaming through the tall windows, the hard benches beneath him, Silas felt a strange sense of peace and security, one he never felt while watching the church from across the street those many times. He drifted off into a seated nap, only awakened perhaps hours later by the light hand of the preacher on his shoulder and the inevitable questions.

'Where's your mama, son? When is she coming back?'

Silas didn't answer the preacher's questions, deciding instead to give him his Gran's name and telephone number. Silas had memorized his Gran's contact information just as Gran instructed him. Always have it ready, she said. His mother didn't like to catch him calling Gran on the telephone. And she never took him to visit her. His Gran just came when she could and didn't stop knocking on the front door until Silas' mother answered it and let her inside. When he was a little boy, Silas associated his Gran with long, unending knocks on the door. Did Gran fear that his mother wouldn't let her in without the knocks, without the broadcasting of her presence up and down the block? After Gran left, his mother would mutter and curse her under her breath. Silas knew these were bad words because Gran told him they were and must never be repeated in "polite" company.

Gran came to retrieve Silas from the church that day. She'd had to leave one of her cleaning jobs, with the work incomplete. But this was an extraordinary circumstance, and the employer had insisted she go. She thanked the preacher profusely for his time and for giving Silas milk and cookies in the rectory and for generally taking such good care of him. When they arrived home, she made Silas his favorite ham and Swiss cheese on rye sandwich.

The bus station could be heard and smelled even before it came fully into view. The motors of buses, the beeping sounds to warn others as they backed out of their spots, the particularly thick smell of their exhaust fumes tightened the knot of excitement in Silas' belly. He was glad of the sounds and smells and jumped out of the truck as soon as Gran had pulled into the station. He unloaded the back of the truck while Gran waited near the suitcases in front of the station building. There was no line of customers at the ticket counter, and the bus station waiting room was nearly empty. Silas saw a homeless man sprawled out on one of the benches and a soldier in fatigues on a seat against the window, his head drooping in slumber towards his chest, his duffel bag on the floor at his booted feet. Near the kiosk, a woman was stationed with a cup in her extended hand. He saw a sign ahead stating "No Idling Permitted" in oversized block black lettering. Clearly, this edict was not being followed. Silas had never thought of a bus station as a place where someone would want to idle, but now that he was leaving all that was familiar to him, he could see its appeal. In serving as a center for transience, the bus station provided shelter, warmth, and potentially, company and food to those whose life conditions were essentially transient, who lived in transience.

Silas approached the ticket counter and requested a one-way ticket. He was surprised it cost less than what he was expecting. In fact, he was surprised there still was a bus station in this town at all, since so many of the stations in nearby towns had shut down. Although she'd let Silas drive it when he was in town, Gran would need her truck here in the country and in town. He'd manage once he got settled.

Gran displayed no emotion when Silas returned outside. Not that Silas was expecting it any other way. He assured her he purchased the ticket and everything was in order. Just as he wished earlier for a dog to complete their leaving the house, Silas wished he could smoke a cigarette now – something to ease the excitement, something to do with his hands. Sometimes, he was as jumpy as his mother, he thought. But Silas and his grandmother were fond of each other's company, and the silence between them wasn't really silence at all, especially with the song of the bus motors, the sounds of the luggage being loaded, and the riders (far more numerous than there were in the station waiting area) showing their tickets to the drivers and boarding the buses.

Silas heard the bus driver call out his destination. And then he felt Gran nudging him to board. Silas wasn't sure how she knew where he was going since he hadn't told her, but Gran told him not to ask. She just knew. The two of them embraced wordlessly. Silas was surprised by the strength of Gran's arms around him and his trembling beneath them. When they disentangled, Gran took his hands in her callused ones and looked at him steadily under the bus station lights as if she wanted to memorize his features and then embraced him again. When he boarded the bus, Silas saw Gran standing there alone now, not waving as she used to do when he boarded the school bus. But just standing there. Silas stared back at her, once blowing a kiss. Gran touched her lips with the underside of her palm in return. As the bus pulled out of the station, as he settled back into the seat, Silas felt he was abandoning her, that he was abandoning Gran, that he was running away from home, from shelter and into storm.

***

Shortly after his arrival in the city, Silas found a job at a vegetarian café. The manager inquired about his restaurant experience and seemed pleased by his tenure at the ice cream parlor and later at a hardware store.

'Customers are customers. As long as you know how to treat them, you can learn how to serve them,' she said.

Silas smiled at this bit of wisdom. The manager was impressed with Silas' quick smile and his easy manner.

'You keep smiling here, son, and you'll do just fine,' she said.

On the employment application form, Silas wrote down the address of the YMCA where he was staying, at least until he got on his feet. He didn't really know anyone in town, although he'd heard some of his friends, other misfits, from high school had moved here. He probably could've called them but he really didn't want to see them. After high school, they'd gone on to college, while Silas stayed on at the hardware store, eventually making his way up to assistant manager. Even though Gran wanted him to further his education, she'd been proud of him when he told her about his promotion at the store. To celebrate, she made him apple pie à la mode for dessert that night.

Working at the natural foods cafe was easy enough. Silas mastered the menu fairly quickly. The patrons, with their various allergies, intolerances, uncertainties, and deeply held philosophies, were uniformly assured in Silas' calm manner. No, nothing was processed; no gluten or animal products had been used. Yes, the lentil burgers, the artisanal multi-grain bread, and the tofu "meat" were some of the restaurant's most popular items. Customers found the seasoning and spices used by the chef to be especially delicious and always compared the menu favorably to the bland vegetarian or health food fare they'd sampled at other establishments. Silas thanked them and conveyed their compliments to the chef, who smiled in return. The chef didn't speak much English, and Silas wondered where he'd learned to cook this way. He wondered whether Mr. Stevens, the manager of the hardware store where he used to work, whose favorite meal was truly the proverbial meat and potatoes, would eat this food. Silas wondered if Gran would enjoy it, whether, despite the seasoning, it would be hearty and balanced enough for her. He wondered whether the chef could teach her to cook this way. Glancing at the food he brought out to the café patrons, Silas thought of Gran's delicious food he devoured on the bus to the city. On that ride, no one requested any food. He even offered the rider next to him some of the bounty, but she declined. He wanted to talk briefly about Gran, to sing her praises, but the rider turned away, leaning her head against the bus window.

The nights in the city were hardest for Silas. Although he liked his room at the YMCA, his sleep was typically fitful. There were loud street noises into all hours of the night – vehicles honking, drunken pedestrians leaving the bars and breaking into fights, bottles crashing on the pavement. Still, Silas did manage to get some rest. Often, it was when he least expected it, when his body was most tense, such as after a truck rumbled loudly in the restaurant loading dock nearby. Silas would realize the next morning that he'd dropped off suddenly, as if from a cliff, into sleep. He would think back to the crickets back home and remember his entrance into sleep then, the slow movement, the fluttering into rural rest.

***

After his Friday shift at the café, which ended at about 10 p.m., Silas went out to the bars. He was still carded all the time, even here in the city. He looked at the men, at the posters of the shirtless muscle studs against the walls. Sometimes, someone would glance his way, and sometimes someone would strike up a conversation with him, about who he was, where he was from, since he was so obviously not from here, with that accent and that … umm … demeanor. But Silas didn't drink at all. He was also naturally shy. At school, he answered the teachers' questions and spent recess reading or dozing at his desk or walking around the school grounds. At home, he spent most of his time with his mother and then his grandmother, neither of whom required much in the way of conversation. And maybe the examples of his mother's male friends, with their thudding steps slipping into lurching, were also in the back of his mind. Sometimes, he felt he was here in this bar because this was what was done, this was where a boy, or young man, as it were, from the country went when he first came to the city. Or so he had somehow heard.

Usually, Silas left the bar after a half-hour or so, excusing himself from a conversation or leaving his empty ginger ale bottle on the bar. He'd walk the streets of the city, as if in a daze, yet always finding himself back at the Y without any problems. He'd call Gran from the payphone, leaning into the glass, cradling the receiver, listening to the sounds of her love that never demanded a response, as the urban nightscape unfolded around him. When someone banged on the door of the telephone booth, Silas wished Gran a good night and quickly hung up.

On such nights, Silas found it difficult to sleep at all. He'd think about his reason for running away, or leaving home. Or rather, the reason would return, unbidden, to him. He'd visualize that day, in his senior year of high school, the first day he saw Jim, or rather the first day Jim appeared to have noticed him. Actually, Silas had seen Jim many times before around school, often going out of his way to look at him, transfixed by his blue eyes, body thick everywhere, including the waist, by the black hair sprouting from massive forearms.

That day, Jim actually looked directly at him and gestured him to follow him into a dense grove of trees, almost a forest really, behind the football field, where Jim played, or more likely these days, sat on the bench, having been jolted out of the starting lineup by a new athlete in the school. When they were far enough into the wood, he gestured for Silas to get to his knees against a tree and keep his hands behind his back. He pulled himself out through the flaps of his white briefs and, already nearly hard, thrust deep into Silas' mouth. Silas exulted in the feel of Jim, in his fullness, in his own bringing of pleasure, even if he was never allowed to touch himself or speak at all. Even Jim's sweat seemed so different from Silas' own – more musky, seemingly from another realm of masculinity altogether. When Jim was finished, when he'd made sure that Silas swallowed by holding the back of his head tightly, he immediately zipped his jeans back up. He told Silas to wait there on his knees for five minutes after he disappeared, through the pine trees, from view.

Silas remained on his knees far longer than the commanded five minutes. Unable to rise, utterly bereft, Silas lowered his head to the ground. After such pleasure never before experienced, now this. Had he ever been so alone? There, he lay in the fetal position, feeling the forest, yes it was a forest, thrum around him. He heard songs from high in the trees and a chorus of murmuring arising from the depths of the earth. He inhaled the fragrances that surrounded him. None of the forest's creatures approached him, but he perceived them their curiosity, their cautious movements, the slightest rustling of leaves just outside his realm of vision. Or was he simply imagining these creatures? And slowly he found his way to rising.

This ritual with Jim, for so it felt, with its unquestioned, repeated procedures and gap between server and served, continued for nearly a year. Silas could never resist Jim's gesture, the slight turning forward of his head. Whenever it came, he was ready. He came to know Jim's schedule and when he was most likely to see him and be seen by him. And if others saw, no one said anything. No one commented or teased or noticed Silas any more than they had before, which was really not much all. Some girls glanced his way from time to time, and a few – Amber and Tiffany – even sent him some valentines. Silas thanked them but did not reciprocate. He was transfixed by

Jim, by the pull of him. No matter how much he told himself he had to stop, that he couldn't keep doing this, that he was worth more, that he was better than this, he couldn't refrain from following Jim into the forest.

Waiting on his knees afterwards, Silas would slowly count the minutes. As his excitement trailed off into loss, he slowly sounded out the numbers. Phrases from Gran's favorite hymn such as "Lord, lift me up" and "Lord, plant my feet on higher ground" that she sang with such relish both at church and at home would float through him, and he would slowly rise (or be lifted) from the black, loamy soil.

Gran was mortified by the plummeting of Silas' grades. He could tell this not by her expressed concern or her asking specific questions, but by her asking him to sit with her in the living room after they cleared away the dinner plates. Sometimes, Silas stayed with Gran in the living room while she knitted, but he couldn't concentrate on the words. And the numbers and equations in his advanced algebra class danced even further out of reach. On other nights, he went to his room and turned off the lights, not to sleep, but to be away from Gran and her concern, and the world itself. Once, when Silas stood up to go up to his room, Gran looked up from her knitting and said, 'Remember, son, the Holy Spirit is inside of you.'

Silas' teachers and his guidance counselor were also concerned. They'd never seen such a precipitous drop in the grades of so promising a student. They were not as reticent as Gran and asked him directly about the cause in this decline. Had something happened at home? In his other classes? Did he understand that admission to college was at stake? Was he still planning on applying to college? The deadlines were looming, and many had already passed. Silas looked down at the floor, not wanting to seem disrespectful or ungrateful, but also not knowing how to respond. These meetings invariably ended in their shaking of their heads or pursing their lips as Silas slunk down the hallway into the tide of students and faculty.

Even Amber, the girl who didn't feel rebuffed by not having been reciprocated a valentine, asked about his well-being. She sometimes brought her lunch tray to his table in the cafeteria. As director of the theater club, Amber introduced Silas to her theatrical friends, but Silas wasn't interested. Even in the best of his school days, he had been more interested in science and math. Theater, with its artifice and staging, didn't compel him. His science classmates didn't ask him any questions, not knowing how to reach out or what to say. Silas had been the one they used to approach with their questions. But now he was so clearly behind the lessons they largely ignored him. His chemistry lab partner, Brian, who covered for him at first, eventually asked the teacher if he could work alone. Amber, on the other hand, didn't seem to mind his silence; she said the theater club meetings provided enough liveliness and noise for her.

Drifting through these encounters and his school days in general, Silas imagined he understood his mother better. How she yearned for the love of the men who came in and out of her life, even as she never seemed to gain it. How she yearned for the love of her mother, Gran, and never seemed to find it. Even at her most defiant and furious, his mother still yearned for it. That day in the Church was the final act of her defiance. She could've delivered him to Gran, but she didn't want her mother to have him. Or rather, she couldn't face her own failure since she knew Gran would get Silas in the end. The preacher would've seen to that. Gran rarely missed a Sunday service. She just couldn't face having to turn over her son, whose paternity was uncertain, to her mother. There wouldn't be gloating but there'd be disapproval. The pursing of Gran's lips marking that disapproval was more than Silas' mother could bear.

Silas did rally somehow to graduate from high school. Barely. Jim called him to the wooded grove just as frequently until the end. But Silas managed to cram before his final exams to score a passing grade in all of his classes. Although he might have been valedictorian, Silas was glad enough to have made it to graduation. Mostly, he was glad for Gran, who cheered loudly from the audience when his name was called and who beamed all day. Snapshots captured that day showcased her glow and smile and Silas' sheepish, vacant grin.

Jim never moved away from town but stayed away from Silas for years after graduation. Silas sometimes overheard snippets of conversation about him in the market or on the town square or read in the local newspaper about Jim's career in law enforcement and his volunteer activities in mentoring underprivileged youth. Silas shuddered to think about the unfortunate souls at Jim's "mercy", caught in the net of his power. Once, when skimming the social announcements in the paper, he saw Jim's handsome face, smiling broadly out at him, as it never had in person, next to the equally broadly smiling daughter of a prominent politician.

If Silas' interaction with Jim had ended there, Silas might well have stayed in town. Only it didn't. Years later, when Jim was a memory in the recesses of his mind, he turned up at the hardware store. When Silas saw him again, his body went into its usual state of betrayal. The married Jim looked almost the same. His cop's uniform hugged his frame more than the jeans and t-shirts or even the jock's uniform. He picked up a few tools and made small talk with Mr. Stevens, allowing his eyes to wander occasionally, almost lazily, over to Silas. He stared at Silas briefly but purposefully. Silas felt himself cower behind the register. As these drop-ins continued, sometimes when Mr. Stevens was out, sometimes when the store was busy, Silas again began to lose equanimity, his balance in the world. A part of his life he thought was behind him no longer was. He wondered if Jim would summon him to another grove or somewhere even more dangerous. And it was soon thereafter that Silas made the decision to leave town, which was a running away of sorts, not from Gran, but from Jim, and another interlude of Jim that might not have ended as benignly as the first, which wasn't benign at all.

***

Lying in his bed in the YMCA, Silas appreciated anew the sentiment, 'The night is still young.' The young night offered him the promise of rest, of a silken obscurity to enfold him. As the night aged, Silas thrashed in restlessness, calling out to his mother, who left him on the church steps in his little boy overalls and to Gran who retrieved him and gave him shelter and barred his mother from him ever since.

Silas summoned his mother and Gran to his late night room, not as he had been summoned to a wood behind a school, but in reparation and in the spirit. He invited them to join him on his narrow bed, even though they were women and this was the YMCA, to put aside their differences, to reconfigure the shards of their love. He invited them to drink from goblets filled with sparkling apple cider, since neither he nor Gran drank alcoholic beverages. He invited them in gratitude for having gotten him this far, to this room, for all they had given him to make him what he was today – a young man of science, if not a valedictorian, who left his grandmother to ride a bus into the unknown. Their faces illuminated in the pink and green glow of the neon "No Vacancy" sign outside, Silas invited them to join him in a toast to his new start in the city. Here, he would find his calling. Here, he had been called.

"Idolatry, Averted"

When Avromi came home from *kheyder* one Friday afternoon, the house was quiet. The entire first floor stretched out before him dark and empty, the wooden boards gleaming with freshly applied polish. Mami wasn't there to greet him at the door, ask about his day, and whisk him into the kitchen for his after-school snack of milk and chocolate chip cookies she had baked especially for him. There were no sounds of his brother Shloymi perfecting his dribble and basketball shot in the alley that ran behind their row home. There were no aromas of cooking emerging from the kitchen, even though Shabbas was only just five hours or so away. And there were no sounds of cleaning anywhere in the house. No vacuum cleaner, no polish of furniture, no popping or spraying of tile.

Avromi wasn't exactly sure when Shabbas started since the clock was changed just last week. But he knew that Shabbas would be earlier than last week. That was what his *rebi* had explained to him earlier in the week. The clock will be different now, he said. Time will be set backwards so you have to move the clock's hands backward. The *rebi* made a backwards motion with his hands. So where was the aroma of the roast chicken? And why was there no soup on the stove? Or gefilte fish in the fridge? Avromi noted these absences as he looked around a kitchen devoid of its usual Friday frenzy.

The inactivity at home was in marked contrast to Avromi's day in *kheyder*. Avromi was selected to lead the class in *Kidesh* and the *ha-Moytse*. He was able to recite both blessings without any mistakes since he practiced many times beforehand during the week with his sister Basye. Even though Avromi heard Tati recite the prayers twice every Shabbas and the *ha-Moytse* often during the week besides, Avromi was glad Basye helped him practice. He really needed it, especially to lead the class. That was because he still didn't really know how to read very well, but he knew the *alef-beys* and could even make out many different words already. The *rebi* reminded him to recite the blessings with *kavone*, which was a little hard for him to do, since the *bekher* was shaking in his hand and the wine kept spilling out over the rim onto his hands and onto the little plate underneath the *bekher*.

Still, the *rebi* said he did well in his recitation. He was able to remember all of the words and the intonation he heard from Tati and that Basye reminded him of during their practice. Only once did he stumble over the words. It was in the *Kidesh* – "*asher bahar banu mi-kol ha-am ve-romemanu mi-kol lashon*" that Avromi stumbled. He just couldn't seem to say the word "*ve-romemanu*". Some of the other boys started to giggle. Avromi felt his face turning red. Not as red as the wine, but still very red. Until the rebi said, '*Ve-romemanu*' for him and said '*Vayter*, Avromi.' And then Avromi was able to finish the blessing all the way until the end. Yes, the whole thing, he would tell his sister when he next saw her, probably without mentioning the "*Ve-romemanu*" part.

After Avromi finished both the *Kidesh* and the *ha-Moytse*, the whole class sat down. It wasn't a real meal, with fruits and vegetables and healthy stuff Mami was always talking about, but it was still festive and therefore good for you, just in a different way. As the students gobbled down the fudge sandwich cookies and the chocolate covered wafers and the ruffled potato chips and trail mix (that was a little healthy, wasn't it?) and as they guzzled the soda and the apple juice, the *rebi* explained that today's party was a way to get ready for Shabbas. It couldn't replace what would happen later at home – how they must and would help their parents cook and clean and always be obedient and helpful *yinglekh* at home and at school and on the street so they could always bring *nakhes* to their parents and joy to *Klal Yisroel*. But still it was important.

With the excitement of his almost-perfect recitation and the treats enjoyed afterwards, Avromi had trouble concentrating on the rest of the day's lesson, which was about the laws of Hanukah menorah lighting. Even though Hanukah was far away, it was the next holiday on the calendar, and the *rebi* felt that here too it was never too early to get ready. His feet dancing off the floor (so that he had to assure the *rebi* he did not have to go to the bathroom), Avromi could hardly wait to tell Basye about his performance and the whole day, too.

That anticipation that had been building up in *kheyder* left Avromi a bit disappointed when he couldn't find Basye at home. Having looked through all of the first floor, even the hiding place behind the living room couch where she sometimes hid, Avromi decided it was time to look upstairs. She must be in her bedroom, he decided. At the top of the staircase, he continued straight (as opposed to making a left turn which went to his parents' bedroom), past the bedroom he shared with Shloymi, to Basye's bedroom. Avromi was prepared to knock on the door because he knew how upset with him she'd be if he didn't. But to his surprise, the door was almost completely open. Instead of knocking (which he for sure would have done had the door been closed or even less open), Avromi called out softly, 'Hello! Hello! Are you in there, Basye?' He stuck his head around the door, his body still in the hallway. But there was nothing out of the ordinary.

If anything, the room looked too perfect. His sister's bed was made, without any indentation in the blankets to show that she'd been sitting there. The lights were off; the shades were pulled down. If Avromi didn't know better, he'd think she just woke up from a nap, made her bed, and went to take a walk or something. But Avromi *did* know her better. Basye wouldn't take a nap on Friday afternoon. She was too old for that, too *mature*, as she liked to say. A Shabbas afternoon nap, of course, everyone took one of those. But Friday afternoon? Never! Anyway, Basye wasn't in her room.

Avromi decided to check the attic next. Well, it wasn't really an attic like the one he'd seen in his friend Sruli's house, which had a bed, a dresser, and a desk and was always kept clean. It was more like a space to put old things that no one wanted or that could be used again "for a rainy day" as Mami once suggested to him. Avromi liked rainy days when he could bake chocolate chip cookies with Mami and Basye. He liked to roll the dough into balls between his palms, round and round, as Mami taught him. He liked to look through the oven window to see the balls expand into cookie shapes, the way they were supposed to. But even before all that, Avromi liked to make sure that all the right ingredients in the right amount were included. That was especially important, Mami said. Especially, the chocolate chips. Avromi loved to pour those into the bowl, enjoying the plunkety-plunk they made when falling into the batter. Or splat-splat if the mixture was very wet. If the chocolate chips fell against the walls of the bowl, they made a clunkety-clunk sound. His mother always let him lick the spoon; he didn't even have to ask. Basye used to enjoy licking the spoon with him. But not so much anymore. Avromi sometimes forgot what exactly he was doing or supposed to be doing. But then he remembered the attic again.

He pushed open the door to the attic. This door was different from the other doors in the house. It wasn't locked or open or even just closed. It was hard to get open, not stuck exactly. His father could open it. Shloymi could open it; Avromi noticed that Shloymi was getting big and strong, especially his arms. He could see this before Shloymi changed into his pajamas. Avromi knew he really wasn't supposed to look, but he sometimes did when he thought Shloymi wouldn't notice. Like when he was too tired after a game. Tati wanted Shloymi to focus more on his *limudey-koydesh*, but Shloymi really liked to play ball. Not just basketball either. Also baseball and soccer.

But there were times when Avromi didn't have to sneak to peek at Shloymi. That was when Shloymi wanted him to look at his muscles. Before putting on his pajamas, he would say, 'Avromi, check these out!' and then tighten his arms so they got very round and big and jumpy and his face would get very red a little bit like the red Avromi felt his face getting today in school when he couldn't pronounce "*ve-romemanu*". But different since Shloymi was smiling and pleased with his arms. He said these parts of the arm were called "biceps" and triceps. Shloymi would point those out, too. Shloymi's triceps weren't as big as his

117

biceps but they could still move on their own and they had "good definition" which pleased Shloymi. Shloymi never let him feel his arms, although Avromi wanted to very much. But he never asked. Avromi knew it wasn't right to ask. He didn't think Shloymi would mind, but Tati would. Avromi knew that for a fact.

The door to the attic was heavy. When he was finally able to open it, he almost lost his balance. He pushed so hard that the door opened very suddenly. Maybe he wasn't as strong as Shloymi but Avromi was still strong for his age. He called out, 'Hello! Hello!' even though the attic wasn't that big. If Basye were in there, she would have heard him. Avromi saw bags of clothes that his mother would be taking to the *Gemakh* soon. Maybe some dresses that she no longer fit into or was tired of or just didn't seem right anymore. Mami said it was important to value everything we have since so many people have so much less and not to want what we didn't have. "Covet" was the word she used. Which was different from "cover" that went on a bed. It was funny how a word that was almost the same could mean something so different. Even though Avromi didn't know a lot of words, he knew his ABC's.

Mami said we should use everything for as long as we could. She said her *bobi* used to tell her that in some place called "The Old Country" they didn't throw away dresses or clothes at all. The people wore them until they had holes in them and couldn't wear them anymore. Even though they lived now in "The New Country", Mami still followed her *bobi*'s example. Rummaging through some of the bags in the attic, Avromi took one dress and held it up to the window. It was gray but it looked like it could have been a different color a long time ago. Holding it up against the attic window, he saw that the elbows were worn thin and there were stains under the arms. This was from sweat, Shloymi explained to him. 'You will sweat some day when you get older,' Shloymi assured him. Avromi wondered who would be able to wear a dress like this gray one in his hand. Even in "The Old Country" the ladies probably wouldn't keep on wearing dresses like this. Maybe it could be torn up and used for *shmates*? He wouldn't ask Mami about it. If something were in these bags, she put them there for a reason. But he would remind her that the attic window needed to be cleaned. Maybe he would surprise her and wash the window himself. But he'd have to tell Mami he washed it since neither she nor anybody else came up here much. And then it wouldn't really be a surprise anymore.

Avromi heard the doorbell ring. Maybe someone had forgotten the key! He put the gray dress back in the bag, took a final look around the attic, and then shut the door behind him. It was easier to shut a door than open it. He called out, 'Coming!' as loud as he could, even though his mother had taught him not to shout and not to run down stairs. Still, this was different. When he finally reached the front door, it was in record time. He was sure of that.

When he opened the door, it wasn't someone from his family. It was Rebetsin Grünwald from a few doors down. She came from a place called Germany, where many Jews were killed. Rebetsin Grünwald had a green number on her arm, which you were not supposed to talk about. Her name meant "green forest", which was where many of the Jews were killed, but not the Rebetsin's family, because they were killed in a *lager*, which means camp. A *lager* was different from a summer camp, where Shloymi was a counselor. In a *lager*, all the prisoners slept squished together and there wasn't enough food and there was hard work and everyone had to stand for roll call in the hot and cold weather in just their thin uniforms. There were even showers that rained poison instead of water.

When Avromi told the Rebetsin his mother wasn't home, she said she just wanted to return a dozen apples she had borrowed a few days ago. 'And please send your mother my thanks and regards. *A gutn* Shabbas, Avromi!' she said before hurrying away down the path. Avromi didn't tell the Rebetsin he was the only one in the house since he wasn't supposed to be left alone. The Rebetsin said her words differently, the way people from Germany said theirs, but not so differently that Avromi couldn't understand them. He just had to listen a little bit harder.

He lifted the bag of apples to his nose and inhaled. Avromi liked the smell of apples. They made him think of trees with flowers and Rosh Hashana and falling leaves. Mami liked to bake something called Apple Brown Betty, which had cinnamon and was crumbly and was different from apple crisp. Unlike chocolate chip cookies, Avromi was not allowed to help Mami bake Apple Brown Betty. Avromi put the bag of apples returned by Rebetsin Grünwald in the fridge. He made sure to close the door, which sometimes stayed open.

If the fridge stayed open for too long, the food would become *farfoylt* and would have to be thrown into the garbage. If that happened, Mami would be very unhappy. And Tati would have to know, which would not be good for anyone, least of all Avromi. *Bal tashkhes*, his father would say, with a frown. And Avromi would probably get punished. Maybe even spanked. *A por petsh*, Tati called the punishment. Only Avromi was sure that it wouldn't just be a few. And Mami wouldn't be able to convince Tati not to spank him. No matter how hard Mami tried to convince Tati not to spank him, even crying when trying. Crying more than Avromi himself, who knew how to hold back the tears, even though his father's hand, which was big, a lot bigger than Shloymi's even, stang on his bare tush since Avromi had to pull his pants down to the floor when he bent over. Sometimes he could hear his belt clank against the floorboards as Tati's hand hit his tush. Avromi used to wear suspenders, but now he wore a belt, like Shloymi and the bigger boys. Basye once told Avromi that suspenders were called "braces" in a country called the United Kingdom, which was very far away, across an ocean. Avromi wondered what people in the United Kingdom called the wires put on teeth to make them straighter. Were they also called braces? He'd have to ask Basye some time.

When Tati made up his mind, it was hard to change it. Even though Mami tried sometimes. Tried a lot. Once Avromi tried to run away from Tati's hand, but the spanking was even worse when he was caught. So now he didn't run away any more.

Making extra sure again that the fridge door was closed, Avromi decided to look in the basement. It was really the only place in the house to look, besides his parent's bedroom. And Avromi was NEVER allowed to go in there. At the bottom of the basement stairs, there was a light switch that was a little too high for him. He could get a stool or jump up to reach it. Avromi jumped up and managed to flick it on.

The basement still seemed dark, even though the light was on. Its walls were gray like cement but not like the gray of the dress in the bag in the attic. More cold, less like dirt. 'Hello! Hello!' Avromi called out, just as he had done in the attic. There was no answer. But Avromi stood very still, not looking around but holding himself still. He could hear someone crying. It was coming from a corner, farthest from where he was standing. Avromi could tell that because he was listening carefully, the way he tried to do when he was most afraid but sometimes couldn't. Only now he was listening.

Walking down towards the sound, Avromi got closer and closer. Finally, he was there. Underneath a wall, which wasn't really a wall, of hooks and screws and dials, Avromi saw his sister. He wanted to shout out, 'Basye, there you are! I've been looking all over for you!' and, 'Basye, why are you lying on the cold floor in the corner of the basement and crying?' Only he didn't. He couldn't. Instead, he got down to the floor with her and leaned over towards Basye. He pulled her up slowly from the ground, thinking that she might not want him to do that. But her body, which was small and light, lighter even than his, even though Basye was three years older than him, was limp in his arms.

And as he brought Basye up into a sitting position, Avromi put his arms around her. He felt her body shake with sobs, bigger than Mami's when trying to stop Tati from spanking Avromi. At first he wondered if Tati spanked Basye also but then realized he probably didn't. Tati said it was a sin to hit girls, or touch them, and that you weren't even supposed to look directly at girls you didn't know in the eyes. He wondered if Basye failed a test in school. But he doubted it. Basye was very good in school, better than Avromi. She always had the highest marks in the class, which made their mother nervous for Basye and Tati disappointed with him and Shloymi since boys could be *talmidey-khakhomim* and girls couldn't.

Even though Avromi knew he wasn't supposed to touch girls, even his own sister, he continued to hold her. His body rocked Basye's, even though it was a little hard to do since she was crying so hard. Avromi didn't ask her questions about why she was crying; he just kept his arms around her as she cried. Basye didn't exactly put her arms around his body but she didn't tell him to stop and she didn't push him away. Avromi wondered how long Basye could keep on crying without getting tired or even just needing to stop a little. He remembered crying a lot once when he was very young. That was when he wanted to stay over Sruli's house but Mami didn't let him. She said Avromi was too little and she didn't want to be beholden to anyone. But even then Avromi didn't cry as much as Basye was crying now.

Slowly, slowly, Basye's crying stopped. Until it was mostly hiccups. And then just raspy breathing. And then just quiet. 'Thank you, Avromi,' Basye said finally. Avromi was afraid she would cry again so he just held her. Finally, Basye explained what happened.

Tati found Basye's secret box of Barbie dolls. She kept it behind the boots and shoes in her bedroom closet. Avromi knew because Basye let him play with them sometimes. Not as much as he would've liked but still a lot. She said Tati went into her room today, which he never did and found them, even though they were hidden and he probably wasn't supposed to be in her room. Basye never found out why Tati was in her room. When she came home today, her dolls were piled on the floor. But they were destroyed. Tati cut off the noses of Basye's dolls from Barbie, who was very grown up and "developed", down to Midge and even Dawn. Their dresses were all torn; their arms and legs were all twisted; their hair had been all cut off. Tati said that the graven image is idolatrous as it is stated in *Shmoys* 20:4 and that he would never allow his daughter to bring idolatry into his home, which was a home where Hashem was served and where *getshkes* were not allowed.

Basye led Avromi up the stairs now to show him what happened, looking around to make sure no one else was around. She opened the door to her room, turned on the lights, and told him to look under her bed. The destruction that Basye told him about was right there before him. Only it was worse seeing them with his own eyes. The hands and legs were disconnected; the heads chopped off. Avromi supposed the dresses were torn off because they weren't modest enough.

Basye was only able to buy the dolls because she saved the money she made from her babysitting and her handy-girl chores like cleaning and reading the *Eyn-Yankev* to Mrs. Goldshmidt who couldn't see so good anymore. Avromi knew without Basye telling him that something precious had been taken from her, that Basye would be different now. Basye said she would keep the dolls under the bed for a while, maybe even bury them, at some point. But right now she just wanted to lie down. After thanking Avromi again, Basye plopped into her bed on top of the covers.

When Avromi left Basye's room, he wasn't sure where to go. There didn't seem to be anyone around. Would they have food for Shabbas? Had something happened to Shloymi? Avromi knew nothing could have happened to Tati, but he wondered if something had happened to Mami. He remembered the nursery rhyme about the old woman who lived in a shoe and had so many children she didn't know what to do … until she decided to leave. Did the old woman come back? Did she fall down the stairs? Avromi couldn't remember. Mami wasn't old and there were only three children in their family, which was small, since Tati wanted more and Mami couldn't, the doctor said.

Sometimes Mami took long walks, very long walks, and no one knew where she was. And whenever she came back, she never explained where or why she went away. Tati got really mad then. Maybe this time she just kept walking and wouldn't come back in time for Shabbas. Or she wouldn't come back at all. Then they'd really be in trouble, the three of them – Shloymi, Basye, and Avromi – with just their father in the house. Even Mami's crying couldn't stop him from getting spanked, maybe he'd get it much worse on his tush with her gone. Much worse than black and blue.

Sitting on the floor of the stairs, Basye in her room, and dolls butchered beneath her bed, Avromi began to recite over and over the *Kidesh* that he mastered with her and recited at school. Rocking, as he'd just done with Basye in the basement. He kept thinking he heard Mami walk up the path, her step light, feet barely touching the pavement, a brown bag of Shabbas groceries supported by her forearm and held against her chest, its top just below her chin.

"Swimming in the Lavender Room"

"I am always going home, always to my father's house."

Novalis (1772–1801)

Zelig hadn't planned on staying the night. Quite the opposite. In none of his previous visits to his father had he ever done that. He always begged off, citing the rigors of his job as a technical services librarian at a small humanities research institute. Still, his father's wife continued to invite Zelig to stay over, despite his just-as-steady refusals. His father himself never pushed his case, despite repeated invitations over the telephone. Usually, Zelig looked down after the apologies and the 'Not this visit, I'm afraid.'

His father's wife would say, 'Your brother stays with us and has lived to tell about it' or 'Why do you have always have to run off?' or 'Maybe next time you'll think about it.'

Although Zelig was merely traveling to a neighboring city, the trip to his father's house required four modes of public transportation and took more than three hours. Fearful of veering off the roads while looking at a landscape or of crashing into a highway railing or of hitting a child running out into the street after a ball or some traffic cue that he might dreamily have missed, Zelig didn't have a car and didn't drive. That he had a license at all was really only because of an instructor who had taken pity on him after he had failed the driving exam twice just after college. Damn those orange cones! To visit his father and his wife, Zelig took the metro from his apartment to the central train station. Then, he boarded the regional rail train, a journey that lasted an hour.

Zelig's fears did not abandon him merely because he was riding a train. In fact, they were amplified. Images of bodies blown to smithereens and strewn severed limbs and carnage caused by a terrorist's bomb always overtook him with varying degrees of intensity whenever riding public transportation. When he saw a toddler sleeping contentedly in a stroller on the train, he visualized her crying for her mother in the aftermath of a detonation, her cheeks creased in panic and need, the smiles of the lime green caterpillars on her stroller's hood transformed into grimaces in the mayhem. But at least he wasn't in charge, at least he wouldn't be the one responsible for bloodshed, as he would be if he were the driver of a car involved in an accident. On public transportation, it was all out of his hands.

And although Zelig knew the likelihood of meeting one's end in a terrorist attack was quite slim, the images, in their tenacity, never lost their power. It would be just his luck to be that unlucky person, the last number in the unlikely percentile. He tried to give himself credit for making himself take this trip, for even getting on the train at all. But what would use would that "credit" be if he were blown to pieces? He would have overcome his "irrational" fears … and for what? To what end? After finding an aisle seat, Zelig struggled to concentrate on the interwar-era English novel about an unmarried clergyman's daughter he was then reading.

After the regional rail segment of the journey, he descended to the platform, where he waited for more than a half-hour (because it was Sunday) for the subway surface train, which he needed to take two stops in the direction of the newly constructed yet retro-looking ballpark. Instead of the game, Zelig thought about the lights and the panorama of the stadium, with its bright scoreboard, the antics of the mascot, the smell of the popcorn and the sense of connection among the fans. Although his father attended games in his childhood and even recalled catching a ball hit by the Babe himself, Zelig never shared the baseball spectator experience with his father. By early adulthood, his father came to believe that watching professional sporting events was, at best, a waste of time and, at worst, idolatrous, worshipping *getshkes*. So Zelig went instead with friends. Once, Zelig and a school friend named Shimen huddled together under the overhang between the two decks of the stadium as late spring rain pelted down, as the lights of the scoreboard, static now but still radiant, gleamed in the deluge. Their bodies brushed only ever so slightly in the wet chill. Their togetherness, or rather nearness, was never remarked on, then or later.

And then after just two station stops, Zelig disembarked the subway surface car and crossed the street to the subway itself, which was actually only partially a subway since it too ran above ground. Here, he waited in the gloom on a platform sparsely populated, listening to announcements, oft repeated but barely intelligible, regarding weekend track repairs and the dangers of pickpockets and terrorists, until the train arrived. 'See something, say something,' the message repeated periodically. But see what? Say what? How would Zelig know when he saw something that warranted reporting?

When the train emerged above ground, he looked out on a city he ought to have known since he studied in a yeshiva there (here!) some thirty years ago. Only the setting flitted by in a whirl of unfamiliarity. Here, a hill dense with trees towering over a newly replenished stream, there a mini-strip with a gas station, a quickie mart, and a taco truck. And a large mattress store, whose wares were always praised on late night commercials that Zelig saw when sleep eluded him. It could have been anywhere. Zelig had to remind himself why he was here, the purpose of the journey: the patriarch at the end of the tunnel.

When Zelig emerged from the train station, a panic gripped him. Would his father remember that he was visiting? He called him on the subway surface line, but the telephone rang without answer. Was his father in the synagogue or the study hall? His wife, now hard of hearing, sometimes used a phone that would transcribe the words spoken by the caller on a display screen. Only Zelig's voice never seemed clear or loud enough to be picked up by the transcriber. Or maybe it was because of the wind or the traffic outside the train station? Zelig was never sure. Sometimes he shouted out his messages to her that he was at

Station X, the closest one to their house, waiting for his father, wondering if his father had gotten the time and the station correctly. Sometimes she heard his precise message, sometimes she didn't. But she could detect that something was amiss by the urgency in Zelig's voice. And so she grew worried about the whereabouts of his father, concerned that he crashed or missed a traffic light change or some other vital signal. Her apprehension over the husband/father bound her to Zelig as nothing else ever had, despite her repeated efforts at building a connection with him, a son from a previous marriage. Zelig could never bring himself to say "stepson" or consider her to be his "stepmother". Nor did it ever escape him that his father, at eighty-nine, could not be dissuaded from driving, while Zelig, at forty-eight, could not be persuaded to drive. Politely, Zelig hung up the telephone, after delivering bland assurances that he was sure that everything was fine.

Zelig then began to pace the station "kiss and ride" area. A rider shouted, 'Hold the bus!' as the bus pulled away from the station. Despite the calls of the would-be rider and those near the bus (including sometimes himself), the bus pulled away. Zelig shrank into himself to avoid the barrage of obscenities that filled the air in the wake of the bus's departing exhaust fumes.

During previous waits for his father, Zelig heard the driver respond, 'Ain't no time' or 'My supervisor gonna bust my butt if I don't keep to that schedule.' Occasionally, the bus did stop and Zelig would see the (not would-be) rider's face light up with relief, break into a mask of gratitude. Today, she would get the potato stew finished on time. Today, she would finish sewing the black dress she was working on with a pattern from Simplicity. Today, her Bible study group wouldn't grow concerned over her delay. Maybe she could even wear the new dress to the study group meeting. Today, the angels were on her side. On previous visits, Zelig enjoyed spinning scenarios about the lives of the bus riders while waiting for his father at the train station. But today he did no such spinning.

Instead, Zelig turned his attention from the station itself to the nearby shopping plaza after which the station was named. Well, not exactly the plaza, but the stop that came before it. In his junior and senior years in yeshiva, he, along with other students, were driven in a school bus on Friday afternoons to swim in the community center. There, Zelig crouched in a corner so that his willowy, hairy nakedness wouldn't be noted (even though it was) and then furtively glided to the shallow end of the pool. Since he couldn't swim, Zelig drifted listlessly, joylessly, his feet touching the tiled floor, drinking in the stink of the chlorine, trying to avoid looking at hair emanating from his body that seemed magnified and even more alien in the pool than it did outside of it. He would treat himself to sidelong glances of the swimmers, his classmates, especially the lithe and muscular ones, on whose forms the hair seemed so well distributed, so reasonable. Only he couldn't look too often or for too long since his insufficiently baggy school bus orange "swim" trunks wouldn't be able to conceal the effects of his longing.

To divert his eye and thoughts from the bodies of his classmates, Zelig forced himself to concentrate on the fact that it was a father's duty to teach his child to swim and that his father reneged on this paternal requirement. At that time, Zelig never considered his inability to swim to be a shortcoming in his own filial performance. Instead, he would rue the foundational moment in which his father had thrown him into the pool and left him there, flapping, sputtering, and still (these many years later) unable to swim. Throughout the years, whenever Zelig drifted by a swimming pool in a local gym or during his travels, the smell of chlorine would always transport him to the bitterness and shame of these Friday afternoons floating in the shallow end of the pool. His *swimlessness*, his state of not-at-swim. Of course, Zelig didn't really require the reminder of the actual chlorine. The odor was etched into his olfactory memory and sometimes arose involuntarily or could be conjured at will.

Seconds before the Friday ordeal was brought to a halt by the whistle, Zelig climbed the steps leading from the pool and was the first into the locker room. He was always the first to board the bus to the shopping plaza, where he could look at clothes that he was forbidden to wear and food that he was forbidden to eat. Was he really now back in this city, waiting at the train station just a few blocks from that plaza of long ago? Had his escape been an illusion?

As the ritual of waiting-for-father-at-the-train station lengthened, Zelig called his sister Brayndl. A woman of valor if ever there were one, or rather the closest he would ever get to a woman of valor of his very own, Brayndl offered a sympathetic shoulder, a pillow to cushion his anxiety. And she had practical suggestions: have you called *Tati*'s wife's daughter or son-in-law? They're bound to know something. Are you standing by the station entrance? Are you near the main road so he can see you or you can see him when/if he drives by?

Of course, with all of these calls, there was the one Zelig could not make to his father. Despite his entreaties (and those of his siblings), his father didn't have a mobile phone. Or rather, he did have one, in fact several, purchased for him by Brayndl, but which he never used. A typical exchange between Zelig and his father went as follows:

'But what if there's an emergency on the road? Wouldn't it be so much easier if you could call me and let me know where you are so that we won't worry?'

'If there's an emergency, *Got vet helfn*. There's no need to worry. We're all in the hands of *ha-Kodesh Borekh Hu*. Besides, I'm too old, and I don't really need it.'

His father's assertions were accompanied by a gesture of open hands and moving back of his hand, the equivalent of a shrug, meaning: We've served God all these years without a mobile phone, and we'll continue to serve Him without a mobile phone.

And then, seemingly out of nowhere, his father appeared at the train station. Instead of an overturned car with a smoking hood, instead of the disfigured or mangled body that he (and his father's wife) envisioned, here was his father, utterly unperturbed. His father's hand, still firm, surrounded and gripped Zelig's own. His beard, once long and plush, now truncated and frizzy, grazed his cheek. Once in the car and on the road, his father's presence exuded welcome, even as he aimed to navigate the traffic flow that proved challenging. Madly, cars and trucks honked at him; drivers gestured obscenely out the windows. Unmoved, his father drove on. *Got vet helfn* indeed.

There was never anything outwardly untoward about Zelig's visits themselves. His father and his wife lived in an apartment built for them by his father's wife's daughter and her husband adjacent to their own home. Everything was modern and easy-to-reach, small but not cramped. The word "*gemitlekh*" floated through Zelig's mind when he crossed the threshold. He was grateful his father had this home with his sacred texts and commentaries and a loving spouse to look after him and that he didn't need to be in an old-age home.

During this particular Sunday visit, his father's wife served a veritable feast: gefilte fish, garden salad, sweet potatoes, coleslaw, and chicken soup, and veggie burgers, too. Some of these were leftovers from Shabbas; others prepared specially for his visit. The veggie burgers were clearly of the latter category. His father's wife moved a bit unsteadily, sometimes holding onto the counter or another surface for balance. She already had several falls, once from a chair on which she was standing to reach a baking bowl needed for a seven-layer cake. Her trembling hands successfully carried the soup to the small peninsula jutting out from the cooking triangle at which Zelig and his father ate. She refused any of Zelig's overtures of assistance to bring over the dishes. Zelig's father knew better than to offer, or perhaps he simply enjoyed being served, as he once did by Zelig's mother, his father's first wife, when his father and his mother were younger.

Zelig's father spoke about the Torah portion of the week, *Va-yera*. His father was particularly intrigued by the *Akedah*, God's commandment of the patriarch Abraham to sacrifice his only son, Isaac.

'Can you imagine the grief? The sorrow felt at the coming loss of the son born to him and his beloved wife in their old age. That is faith,that is true *emune*, the bedrock on which *Klal Yisroel* lives.'

As his father spoke, his fist shook up at the kitchen light fixture. Zelig, who usually just listened to his father, made a rare offering.

'All these years, thousands of commentaries obsessed over and dissected over the millennia, and we're still no closer to understanding this passage. Its meaning eludes us, *Tati*.'

'No, Zelig. Its meaning is right there in front of us. *Moyredik*! We understand it very well. Only by sacrificing everything can someone ever hope to achieve what is real, what is true. That is the key to the survival of *Klal Yisroel*.'

His father's wife hovered in the background, having declined to partake in the feast or the discussion. She sat on the sofa and thumbed through back issues of the English-language weeklies and monthlies of the ultra-Orthodox press. Zelig wondered if she was listening as she was reading or just listening. He knew she wasn't just reading; some element of listening was at work.

A hagiography of his father's mentor (and the man after whom Zelig was named) was on the coffee table in front of the sofa. His father pointed it out to him on a previous visit. Zelig perused it briefly, noting the blend of piety and politics. One anecdote in particular detailing how the rabbi had refused to appear on a dais with representatives of the more liberal (i.e. "impure") branches of Judaism stayed with him. Despite the love of books Zelig cultivated so meticulously in both his professional and personal lives, he and his father simply read different books. And even if they read the same books, they read them differently. In the unlikely event that Zelig ever read the hagiography he would be interested in what it revealed about the cultural norms of the community in which he was raised and which he long ago departed. Any strict belief in the ideal, laws and precepts espoused in the book (or any of the other religious ones lining his father's shelves) was completely out of the realm of consideration. And yet given his extensive religious instruction, Zelig did not place himself outside the imagined community of religious readers. He never knew where he'd find himself on the insider/outsider continuum. Most days of late it was on the outsider end. Today where was he?

His father's wife stood up to ask them intermittently if they'd had enough (as if not having had enough was even an option!), to clear away the dishes and put them in the dishwasher or to put utensils and food away or to hover otherwise about.

Zelig wasn't really sure. He was aware of her chiefly as a presence, not exactly an audience to this passion(less?) play. Her opinion, if she ever chose to express it, might emerge later, months or years later, seemingly off-handedly, as in a visit years before when she chastised Zelig for not calling his father on *erev* Shabbas. It is a child's duty to call his parents before the Sabbath, she then said to him.

And yet for all her hovering today, Zelig was aware of the centrality of his second wife in his father's life. Today, as always, the deep love and ease of being between his father and his second wife were palpable. Did his father love her more than he loved Zelig's own mother? Surely there was room for more than one romantic love in a person's life. Right? … Had the fact that they married in their mid-sixties meant that their expectations had shifted? That compromise and flexibility were easier? That they cared less about the small things? Had his father mellowed with age when it came to the domestic realm? That Zelig doubted. He certainly hadn't relaxed when it came to Zelig, regularly insisting he marry a woman, although Zelig repeatedly assured him that was not going to happen. Was the second wife stronger, more confident, more comfortable in her skin and more insistent on her way than the first? Or perhaps Zelig had it all wrong. After all, he didn't live in his father's home, and except for these brief visits and family occasions, rarely saw the couple. What did he know of their true relationship? Perhaps he was idealizing it from the outside. Of course, Zelig would never ask his father these questions. He heard from Brayndl that his father and his wife purchased side-by-side cemetery plots in The Holy Land. Was this act alone the revealing answer to his questions, the one that rendered the asking irrelevant, unnecessary?

His father's wife's daughter Libi entered at this point. Her own home was separated from his father and his wife's apartment by only a single door. Libi asked her mother what kind of raisins were best in a *lokshn kugl*. Her mother assured her that golden raisins were the best since they didn't disturb the color or the taste of the *lokshn* itself. Libi said how good it was to see Zelig,that he must stay with them for a Shabbas some time. With Libi's sudden appearance, Zelig envisioned this apartment as the set of a sit-com, the various players popping in and out for comic effect. Jack and Janet and Chrissy and the Ropers. *Come and knock on our door ...*

As he and his father lapsed into silence after Libi's exit, Zelig was struck by the gusto of his father's appetite. In old age, he appeared to savor the pleasures of food more than ever. Growing up, Zelig always thought of his father as an exemplar of restraint when it came to pleasures of the palate, confining himself largely to fruits and vegetables and proteins and whole grains. He remembered the granola his mother made for his father, the cluster of oats, nuts, and honey. Had there been raisins too? He remembered the yogurt she made for him, covering the cups with a special cloth in the yogurt machine, never adding fruit or other flavors. That had been his father's breakfast then: granola and plain yogurt crafted by his mother. The potatoes of his mother's *tsholnt* had been the principal starch that his father had allowed himself. Only now Zelig wasn't sure. Perhaps how his father ate now was how he'd always eaten. Perhaps Zelig got it wrong all this time.

As their meal wound down, as his father's wife cleared the dishes (having refused again his offer of help), his father said it was time for *minkhe*. There wasn't an implicit invitation or question, nor was it an announcement per se. It was simply that time of day. Usually, Zelig accompanied his father to the nearby synagogue, where he knew no one and could expect no inquiry or interrogation. If he were noticed at all, he would be a stranger in their midst, a Jew landed unsurprisingly in a house of prayer. There, Zelig could enter the rhythm of the service, whose words were inscribed for time immemorial, whose cadences and melodies never failed to connect him to that which he had been and now could no longer be, no matter how much his father wanted it and no matter how lovely this unencumbered afternoon service (before his father drove him back to the train station) actually was.

Only this time, Zelig declined the call to prayer. What got him to go into the guest room, to cross that threshold, was unclear to him. Perhaps it was the seemingly interminable wait at the platform of the last leg of the journey. Perhaps it was the jitters of being so long on public transportation. Perhaps it was the dire vision of catastrophe narrowly averted. Perhaps it was the bounty of food only just imbibed. Perhaps it the discussion with his father inspired by the weekly Torah portion. Perhaps it was the flood of memories of long ago. Perhaps ...

Overcome by fatigue, enervation even, Zelig asked if he could lie down. His father's wife assured him that he was more than welcome to do so, that there was clean linen there for him. Murmuring his thanks, uttering assurances that all was well, that they needn't worry, Zelig left them in the main kitchen/living/dining room. As he closed the door to the guest room, he heard his father's goodbye to his wife, his shuffling but steady gait to the door, and finally the closing of the door on his departure.

The lavender hue of the guest room walls did not live up to its reputation of restfulness. Zelig tossed and turned on the one of the twin beds. Of course, much of his exhaustion, he realized, could have been avoided if he'd splurged and taken a cab from the train station to his father's house. And while he technically could have afforded it, Zelig didn't feel the expense was justified on the meager salary he earned as a librarian at a small humanities research institute. More importantly, Zelig realized he'd actually sought out this exhaustion, that somehow it seemed appropriate, necessary even, for his entrée into his father's apartment and his return to this city where his isolation had first crystallized, assumed the structure it retained, with some minor variations, to this day.

Sighing inwardly, Zelig returned to the novel that he'd brought with him, curious to know whether the clergyman's daughter love would be reciprocated. But Zelig glanced at the words uncomprehendingly, unable to concentrate. Sometimes he looked over at the empty bed separated by a nightstand from the one he was on. He wondered which of his father's wife's children or many grandchildren had slept in these beds. Briefly, he envisioned his brother Zevulun, ten years his senior, sleeping in this room, racked by a combination of duty and fury and love and guilt over visits that were as infrequent and brief as Zelig's own. Not for the first time did he think about how unusual it was to have two siblings whose first names began with the letter "z". Zevulun and he used to talk about this many years ago, especially when they shared a bedroom when Zevulun was visiting home from his yeshiva in the distant North. But this was not the time to think about his brother. There would be other times, of that Zelig was certain. And so Zevulun exited the lavender room and from Zelig's mind … if only for now, Zelig reminded himself again.

Zelig insisted to himself that he wouldn't think about his inadequacy as a son. He wouldn't think about how he never learned to swim, how he failed to master driving. He wouldn't think about how he failed to be fruitful and multiply, as was explicitly commanded in the Torah itself (and not derived by the Sages may their memories be for a blessing). He wouldn't contrast his own failure with his father's success as a progenitor as manifested in numerous grandchildren and great-grandchildren, many of whom called him far more often than Zelig did. He wouldn't think about the essential evanescence wrought by his childless condition. Here one day, gone the next without a trace. Poof! Was that the origin of the word "poofter"??

Nor would he think about the inadequacy of his visits, with their meager minutes – a meal shared, words of Torah interpretation imbibed/contested, a single prayer service. Surely Zelig visited his father and his wife when he could, had "given" what was possible, given his work schedule, even without children or a wife (or even a partner) of his own. On most evenings, Zelig returned from a day of problem solving and answering correspondence and dealing with patrons at work so utterly depleted that all he could do was stare slack-jawed at the bile of the day billowing from the television: the polarized electorate, the gridlocked government, the climate changing for the worse, etc.

Sometimes, for respite, he watched the competitive cooking shows, drawn by the elaborate dishes with the most improbable ingredients that he, who lived on salads and take-out, would likely never eat and would certainly never prepare, and the personal stories that led the chefs into the kitchen: years of youth spent in addiction, the parents who pleaded/commanded that they go to law school, the sibling with a rare, sometimes incurable disease, the dream of visiting the grandmother who had functioned as mother still living in the islands and unseen for fifteen years. Munching on salads rendered edible with hummus or seeds as the cooking contests marched mercilessly through their winnowing process, Zelig imagined himself a solitary pigeon gazing voyeuristically on tourists sipping espresso or spooning gelato in an Italian piazza at dusk.

He wouldn't think about the chasm between his father and himself, despite their shared love of words and books and study and textual engagement. Today, he wouldn't worry about the train not taken or the fact that he didn't have *tefilin* here for the morning prayer service if indeed he ever did make it through the night and find sleep. Briefly, he wondered if he would remember how to don the *tefilin* correctly. I could Google it, I suppose, if it came to that, Zelig assured himself, becoming increasingly drowsy.

Somewhere in this fog of "wouldn'ts", murmuring voices, afternoon approaching twilight, and lavender, Zelig thought of his mother. He hesitated to say that she came to him. It seemed instead that he could see her finally, in this most unlikely of settings, in the home designed and paid for by the daughter and son-in-law of the woman who replaced her in her husband's affections. Even in this state of semi-sleep, he knew he was not being quite accurate. *Followed* him in his father's affections would be a more apt description, Zelig reminded himself (again).

He saw his mother as a woman of beauty, even into middle age, with her diabetes and her furtive binging in the locked freezer containing her famed chocolate chip cookies, lady fingers, *Levelesh*, and chocolate covered peanut butter squares. All of his mother's treats, he told himself (pettily) were far superior to his father's second wife's seven-layer cake and all had contributed to her fall and arguably her fatal decline.

Zelig remembered his mother's yearning for flowers and romance from a husband who gave her neither, despite her repeated requests, pleas, entreaties, and exhortations. He remembered her seclusion for weeks in their room after a particularly bitter quarrel, one in which neither voices nor hands were raised. A newcomer might have been hard-pressed to note any difference in the house were it not for a particular straightening of the bodies of the key players, a thickening sulfuric ash in the air. And then later, the changes became all too apparent, with his mother's retreat into chamber and the meals, especially the Shabbas meals eaten in silence, her place empty at the table.

And on this night, during this visit to the home where his father now lived without her and in which he had no personal history, Zelig saw his mother emerge from her seclusion. He could feel his childhood self tingling with relief, as the tension lifted, however warily, as life crept back to normalcy, or at least to what was or could possibly be considered normal or every day. Zelig remembered how his mother returned to her work with a kind of incremental gusto, building confidence with each new task completed. Food and greenery blossomed again under her touch following her return. For yes, the plants in the windows had drooped while awaiting her ministrations. 'Always speak to the plants, they need our voice as much water, soil, nutrients, and sunlight,' his mother insisted to him once after emerging from seclusion. He remembered her leaning into him on that day of emergence, her fingers over his tracing the patterns of a towering snake plant, whispering, almost chanting, 'If flowers, as the poets insist, are fueled by love, plants obey a call even more basic, having to do with survival, the will to live itself.' She said all of this to him on the staircase, where he was waiting for her, as he always did throughout her interlude of seclusion.

When she finished these words, when the speaking was over, she led him down the stairs into the kitchen, where she prepared him a snack of a clementine and two oatmeal cookies in purposeful quiet. Zelig noticed the veins in her hands and the firmness of her grip as she placed the treats on the table in front of him. And even though she didn't look at his face, her hands fluttered around Zelig: on his yarmulke, his shoulders, his back.

And here Zelig remembered his visits to the hospital over the years as her decline accelerated. He heard himself conjugating the German verbs he had been studying at the time next to the sick bed so that German always remained for him coupled with death, not because of its connection with "*Schnell!*" or "*Jüden raus!*" or "*Arbeit macht frei*" but because of gleaming white floors and tubes into body and the flickering of monitors with their green graphs and television game shows babbling overhead and body and spirit that would not heal. *Ich bin, du bist, er/sie ist* …

And here Zelig felt the lavender walls embrace him finally as his mother appeared in all of these phases at once in succession and simultaneity, and yet as someone new, different, not changed exactly, but now somehow realized. He felt her hand grip his, not to do away with his grief unexpressed all these years nor to lighten that grief nor even to allow it some expression. Here Zelig glimpsed his mother in her fullness, head in wig and in kerchief, mopping the kitchen floors and in Shabbas repose, talking to plants and to lady friends, knitting needlepoints, murmuring the Psalms. Here he caught sight of her in the range of her activity that he knew and in ways that he never witnessed or even imagined, ones that lay beyond the edges of lavender now streaking finally into blue.

Zelig knew he would forget this cacophony, this panoply of images upon awakening. But here in sleep, in dream, in this state of he knew not, Zelig was a son inadequate no longer. Here, in this room where he never before tarried, his mother appeared to Zelig, not soothing away his fears, but accepting them somehow. Here, she bent to touch his anxieties and inabilities, not to conjure them away, but to caress them, to embrace the nether regions of his Zelig-ness. Here, Zelig reached for his mother; here, Zelig swam at last towards her. In this lavender room, Zelig's mother remained with him in rest.

"Love in the Red"

Yente climbed the stairs – three flights of them – huffing and puffing, like the wolf of the fairy tale she somehow knew from childhood although it was never read to her or allowed into their home. Only this building would not be blown in. Although it had seen better days, it was solidly constructed, probably at the turn of the last century, she thought. The paint in the hallways was peeling. The floors were warped in parts. Most of the light sconces were empty or had bulbs long since burnt out. And besides the expected cacophony of cooking smells, a rank stench permeated the building. Something not skunk-like, but not quite human, either. A noxious chemical odor. Did odor rise, like heat? Yente wondered.

Of course, if this building wouldn't blow in (or down), neither was Yente a she-wolf. Or at least, on most days, she didn't think she was. But today, tucking some of her white hairs under a wig before the bedroom mirror that same morning, she'd seen her worn face, her brow etched in furrow, the wrinkles especially pronounced around her mouth. Perhaps my face does resemble a canine muzzle of some kind, she admitted to herself. Not that it mattered much these days. *Not at my age.*

Yente certainly would never have revealed such thoughts to her husband, Reb Motl, the head (and founder) of a small yeshiva focusing on advanced Talmudic studies. He would have scoffed at such vanity; her appearance was to be circumscribed by the dictates of modesty. A woman's duty was to deflect the eyes of men, not attract them. She was to look after her health so she could serve her husband and God with strength and focus. Reb Motl was an expert on issues of women's modesty and purity. His magnum opus was on the latter topic and included extensive commentary on the Talmudic tractate *Mikvaot*, on ritual baths, and numerous laws governing women's menstrual cycle and its ramifications for her husband and family. A second edition of the volume had recently been released with little fanfare but with considerable satisfaction on the part of Reb Motl, who had toiled for years over the revisions. Although Yente lacked the training to read her husband's writings, she was pleased they were published and proud of his erudition and role in the yeshiva. She enjoyed her role as his helpmate and was adept at running the household and helping in the community.

In general, Yente agreed with her husband on matters of modesty. She never purchased make-up, however discreet in shade. Her dresses were always suitably decorous, with sleeves extended below the elbows, hems dropped far below the knees, and collars high enough to cover the neck. Even before her marriage, she never wore bright colors, favoring black, brown, gray, lavender, navy or midnight blue, and the like. That habit continued after her marriage, although black became her primary color.

It was on the rare occasions when Yente went outside her community that she became the most self-conscious of her appearance. If today, prior to climbing these many flights of stairs, she thought of herself as a wolf, on some days she thought she most resembled a large black bird. Her shapeless black dresses, sometimes overlaid in a smock or a sweater, her sensible black shoes, a black hat covering her wig all conspired to create that impression. Maybe a raven or a crow? Certainly not a grackle since she lacked their flashes of color. Yente saw herself in this way when she saw other women going about their lives, wearing any color of their choosing. She couldn't see herself in the clothes of these women nor did she want to wear them per se. But next to the shades of gold, green, mustard, orange, pink, purple, and teal, among a million others, she became very aware of herself, in a way that she never was when in her community setting. She had to remind herself of her goals and her mission in life as so often reiterated by Reb Motl. Even on the streets of her neighborhood, where she saw women in brightly colored clothing, she never gave them a second glance or thought.

Yente's forays outside the community occurred when she had to purchase something not readily available closer to home or when she was involved in a charitable mission. Even her doctors and dentists were members of her community.

Yente looked up and saw only one short flight of stairs remaining. But she needed to stop and rest. Yente tried to involve herself in charitable work whenever possible. Now that it was just she and Reb Motl at home and now that his yeshiva was on solid footing, her involvement in charity work had become more regular. Yente realized she had quite a few missions to take care of in the next day or so. When she thought about the word "*tsedakah*", she realized that "charity" didn't convey its nuances. It was a word without a real English-language equivalent. Yes, it meant "charity", but it also meant "justice" and "righteousness". Its root was used in many words, including *tsadek* and *tsedeykes*. Hmm ... Tomorrow, she would bring kosher food to the sick in the hospital. But today she had to face what was awaiting her at the top of this last flight of stairs.

Having rested for several minutes on the landing, Yente reached her destination. She knocked on the door, which she noted lacked a mezuzah. Efroyem, her youngest, opened the door. Despite having prepared herself emotionally beforehand, Yente had to restrain her shock. She hadn't imagined that Efroyem would be this far gone, that she would be this late. His cheeks were hollow and pale; his scalp was devoid of all hair. His body, once so slim and willowy, now seemed to be devoid of flesh entirely. For his part, Efroyem didn't seem surprised at all. Mother and son embraced across the threshold, and then Efroyem waved Yente into his apartment.

Only it wasn't really much of an apartment. Yente looked around and saw a single room that included a bed flanked by night tables, a kitchenette, a table with two chairs, a bookcase mostly filled with underwear and clothes, and a desk. There wasn't even a sofa. Yente saw that the bed was really a futon and presumably was raised in upright position when Efroyem had guests or otherwise didn't need it as a bed. Those days were obviously long gone. Even opening the door for her seemed to have taken a toll on him; his breath came in jagged wheezing. Or maybe it was always like that these days? She'd find out.

Yente didn't learn about her son's illness, let alone its advanced state, until a few days ago. She was working with women in the *khevre kadishe* as they prepared the body of a deceased member of the community for burial, a Mrs. Goldfarb, whom Yente had heard of but didn't know personally. After years of involvement, Yente was recently made head of the *khevre*. She found comfort and purpose in the work, and she relished the solemnity of the time and the importance of the task. Yente also felt that the work of preparing the dead for burial called purification was connected to the purity maintained in life that was so thoroughly studied by her husband. Through this shared focus on purity and purification, she felt that her bond with her husband was somehow deepened. Yente and the women in attendance washed the body from head to toe, verifying that there were no medical devices, recited the blessings for the occasion, and placed it in shrouds. After their time with the body had concluded, as they readied themselves to leave, Yente's colleague in the *khevre*, Tsirl said to her:

'I'm so sorry to hear about your son's sickness. I can just imagine how hard it must be for you. My colleague's son also had it when he was young, and there was very little they could do for him.'

As the room and even the corpse began to spin ever so slightly, Yente thanked Tsirl for her support and walked her home per their custom. As she walked the few remaining blocks to her house, Yente wondered how she could help her son. She didn't even pause to wonder what his illness was; she assumed she knew.

***

'Please take off your coat and sit down. I wish I had something to offer you. But you can't really eat from my kitchen. I have some nuts. Can you eat those? Maybe some water? I have some plastic cups.'

143

'A cup of water would be fine, Efroyem. No nuts. Thank you.'

While Efroyem filled a plastic cup with water, Yente removed her coat and sat on a chair by the table. When she visited the home of Gitl, her eldest, and her husband, Eli, she always knew what to do. Immediately upon entering their home, she would discuss with Gitl the latest accomplishments of her seven children. Gitl's eldest, Moyshe, celebrated his bar mitzvah a few months ago. They discussed favorite recipes, home remedies for the children's ailments, and the news of the neighborhood. Just last week, she shared with Gitl a new recipe for fruit bread with cranberries and walnuts. Her grandchildren milled around Yente, basking in her attention and interest and pillowy embrace. In Gitl's home there was a place for her. But here, she felt at a loss. What was she doing here? How many years had it been?

'So how long has it been, Ma? Twenty-one years?'

Efroyem's questions eerily echoed her thoughts. She nodded in assent. Yes, it had been twenty-one years. She remembered the evening well. She had cooked a supper of fried cod and green beans. It was the summer after Efroyem graduated *mesivte*. Graduation had never been assured. Although he'd never been more than a mediocre student, Efroyem's grades in his senior years had become terrible. Despite repeated warnings from his teachers in both sacred and secular studies, he seemed barely present. He wasn't cutting class or getting into trouble with other students. His classes just didn't engage him or otherwise hold his attention. His father tried to find out what was wrong but Efroyem never answered him. Instead, he sat in the chair opposite him, averting his father's gaze and staring out the window. At the end of supper that summer night, he said:

'Ta, Ma, I'm gay. I'm gay. Homosexual. I've known since I was a little kid. And now I want you to know.'

Reb Motl's face turned a color that was both ashen and purple. Something volcanic seemed to rise from his depths. It looked as if all the years of disappointment that his only son had failed to follow in his footsteps and lacked the discipline or the will to live the life set forth by *Khazal* were now bubbling to the surface. Reb Motl never spoke of the shame he must have felt as the head of a selective yeshiva with a son so seemingly undistinguished in Torah learning. He never framed it that way, but Yente imagined that was how he felt. Something was different that night. Reb Motl slammed his fists on the table (Yente remembered the fork clattering on his plate) and shouted, 'Get out! Get out of my house!'

Efroyem did just that, despite Yente's pleas to Reb Motl to allow him to stay and to Efroyem not to go, at least not tonight. Reb Motl had never before raised his voice to Yente or to either of their children. And after this one outburst, he didn't raise his voice again. Nor did he repeat his commands. His response to Yente's pleas was a raised right hand in the air to signify 'No more!' and a turning away of his head. He left the table, went into his study, and closed the door. When she saw Efroyem at the front door with a single suitcase and his backpack, she begged him one final time to stay. But it was no use. She was caught between two *akshonim*. Efroyem walked out of the door and their lives.

Yente finished her glass of water, as Efroyem returned to bed. Now that she was here, there was so much she wanted to ask him. Not to "make up for lost time" but just to know, to learn about her son. But Efroyem seemed tired or spent. Yente sat with him for several hours and then returned home.

***

When she returned the following week, Yente felt better prepared. Her climb up the three flights of stairs seemed far less arduous, even with the packages of chicken and vegetable soup, multi-grain bread, and garden salad she'd made that day and brought for Efroyem. This time, the apartment door was opened by a woman who looked to be about her son's age.

'You must be Ephraim's mother. I'm Summer.'

Yente smiled in greeting at this improbable name. But then who was she to talk? Her name meant "gossipy woman". When Yente was six years old and taunted in school for her name

145

(Yente shmente! Yente shmente!), she asked her mother why she gave her that name.

'It was my *bobi*'s name.'

'But why was your *bobi* named that?' Yente insisted.

'Get ready for supper and don't pay any attention to the teasing. Yente is a fine Yiddish name, and you should be proud of it,' her mother said, pounding the chicken cutlet with added force, it seemed to Yente.

More recently, a temporary receptionist once at the dentist's office had asked her:

'Is the name Yente the same as Yentl like in the movie?'

'Yes, Yentl is the diminutive form of the name Yente.'

'I love the movie *Yentl*. It's one of my all-time favorites!'

Yente smiled and nodded vaguely, hoping to bring the encounter to a graceful conclusion. She hadn't seen the movie (as quite a few of her acquaintances had "secretly" done), although she had been and remained curious about it. Watching movies was strictly forbidden by community norms. Yente once planned to track down the original Yiddish short story by Isaac Bashevis Singer, which was also forbidden, but perhaps slightly less so since it was a written text and not a movie. But somehow she never did get around to it or perhaps never could bring herself to get around to it.

Yente followed Summer into the apartment and went to the kitchenette to heat up the soup and plate the bread and the salad. Summer set the table and helped Efroyem from the bed to the table. Summer complimented Yente on the meal; Efroyem nodded in agreement, although he ate very little of it. The three made conversation, mostly about Efroyem's health and medicine regimen and Summer's work as the director of a gallery specializing in photography. After Summer and Yente finished clearing away the plates and washing the dishes, Efroyem returned to his bed and said:

'Ma, this probably isn't going to be a long reunion. I don't have much time left. I know it's just your second visit, and I don't want you to freak out. I'm glad you came to see me. But I want you to know what happened to me after Ta kicked me out of the house that summer after graduation. It won't take very long.'

Yente nodded for Efroyem to proceed and then assured him that she wanted to hear what he had to say. Summer interjected and said:

'It was great to meet you, Mrs. Koplewitz. I have to run. I have a full day of meetings with artists tomorrow, and I have to get ready. And I'll see you, Mister, just as soon as I come back.'

After Summer left the apartment, after they could hear the clicking of her high heels fade away, Efroyem turned to his mother and, in a monotone punctuated by coughs and laced with hacking, began his story. Yente wondered which was the greater factor in the generation of these terrible sounds: the effort of speaking or the content of the telling. She almost wanted to ask him to stop as soon as he began. Even after twenty-one years, she wasn't sure she was ready to hear this. But she didn't stop him. She couldn't.

The night Reb Motl kicked him out of the house, Efroyem went to a bar in the city. He'd gone there before and, since he looked older than his eighteen years, had never been "seriously" carded. He stood in a certain section of the bar with the others, where he would be appraised in a certain way. Looking, looking away. He wasn't practiced but he knew a thing or two. After several hours, an older gentleman, clearly of means, approached, introduced himself as Kevin, and began speaking with him. About ten minutes into the conversation (after being assured he was of age), Kevin invited Efroyem to return home with him. Efroyem was relieved to be invited. If Kevin hadn't invited him, he might have ended up on the street.

Kevin's home was a townhouse located on a quiet uptown street. A corner house with many windows, it was sparsely but elegantly furnished, where everything was chosen for maximum impact. Efroyem could tell Kevin thought a great deal before purchasing each piece, none of which matched but all of which somehow worked in harmony. Kevin told him to go to his bedroom and strip naked. He joined him in bed a few minutes later. Efroyem told Yente that it hurt but not as much as he thought it would. Lying on the expensive (silk?) sheets of a strange man, Efroyem remembered wishing he were in his bed in the old neighborhood, listening to Yente tidying the kitchen and Reb Motl speaking with students or other rabbis. Of course, when he lived at home, he wished he were elsewhere.

The next morning, Kevin said he could stay here as long as he wanted. He'd need to take care of the house or get a job or go to school. Efroyem had no interest in school and didn't know what kind of job he could get so he stayed in the house. He supposed he was what was known as a "kept boy". He learned to clean and to cook, realizing that he arbsorbed a lot more of Yente's cooking process than he thought. Sometimes Kevin asked him to clean in the nude or in a thong or in boxer briefs or clingy shorts that Kevin bought especially for Efroyem. Kevin liked to see Efroyem bend over in those, which was fine with Efroyem since he preferred that over what happened in the bed itself. Kevin especially liked to run his hands over Efroyem's ass cheeks under the shiny fabric or give them a light slap. Often that was enough for Kevin. Terms like dignity and respect were not of paramount importance to Efroyem during this time. What mattered most then was survival and safety. Kevin never beat him or did anything against his will, and for that Efroyem was grateful.

At this point, Efroyem said he was tired and needed to rest. His mother sat with him on the chair by his bed. She wished Efroyem had a rocking chair. She wished she'd learned to embroider, knit or crochet, something to keep her hands busy. Although her mother taught her to make dresses and darn clothes, Yente never learned the finer arts of the needle. She sat with Efroyem for another half-hour, spread a second blanket over him, and let herself out of his apartment.

***

'Where were you? Why where you out so late at night?' Reb Motl asked Yente as she returned from Efroyem's apartment. She'd entered the house quietly and thought she was in the clear since Reb Motl was in his study.

'I was being *mevaker holim*,' she replied, grateful that she didn't have to lie in this case.

Not suspecting anything, Reb Motl didn't press for details. Why should he? Yente's activity with the ill and the dead was vital in the community. If she were needed at home to tend to him, his students, and other guests, they would manage. Yente always made sure there were enough refreshments for guests in the refrigerator. She always had fish, chicken, a salad, and a *kugl* of some kind, usually potato, on hand.

The next day she brought some of that food to Efroyem's apartment. Although Efroyem ate very little of the food she'd brought during her previous visit, Summer or his other guests could certainly enjoy it. A strange man opened the door and let Yente in. He introduced himself as Steve. Several other guests had already been that there day. Yente saw that they'd left food of their own on the countertop. The refrigerator was already nearing capacity. She had to restrain her instinct to clean and neaten it. At first, she thought it would be best to place the kosher food in a separate area but then realized that it probably didn't matter. Yente didn't imagine that there would be very many guests here observance of the laws of kashrut. Efroyem was dozing, but Steve accepted some chicken and *kugl* that Yente heated and served him.

During his meal, Steve explained that he had worked with Efroyem for years at a volunteer organization delivering food to people with terminal illnesses. He spoke highly of the history of the organization and its overall mission. But he reserved the highest praise for Efroyem himself.

'Ephraim was always the quickest at peeling potatoes and was always ready for the clients with a joke and a smile. He should have been a social worker or a nurse. He had such a great bedside manner. He missed his calling.'

Yente smiled in response. She noticed that Steve was already speaking in the past tense. She really wanted to ask Steve what Efroyem's most recent job had been but she stopped herself. She figured she'd find out soon enough if Efroyem or someone else wanted to tell her. Efroyem's re-entry into her life did not seem to be about her seeking information about him but about that information coming to her. Whatever she was meant to know, she would know. It was God's will, after all these years.

'Thank you for this delicious food. Thank you for being here,' Steve said and exited quietly about a half-hour after Yente's arrival.

Efroyem woke up after an hour and smiled when he saw Yente sitting next to his futon. After declining Yente's offer of food, he sat upright and immediately returned to where he'd left off in his life story at his previous visit. About eight months into his stay, Kevin tired of Efroyem. He didn't say that exactly, but that was the gist of it. Something about 'it was time for Ephraim to move on.' He said he'd found him a job as a personal assistant to a socialite in the same neighborhood named Sophia Gibbons. Her home was furnished in tones of beige, cocoa, and taupe. Despite the neutral color scheme, there was little of the understatement of Kevin's. Like the pillows and lamps, the furniture was oversized. And none of it was very comfortable. Ms. Gibbons was also incredibly demanding, filling Efroyem's every waking moment with mundane, tedious tasks, including laundry, shopping, cleaning, taking her phone calls, fetching the dry cleaning, walking the poodle, among many others. She allowed him no breaks except twenty minutes for lunch. Efroyem found himself longing for the minimal demands of Kevin's household, even with the hands roaming over his ass cheeks under those ridiculous shiny shorts or in the thongs.

Once he found work washing dishes in a Mexican restaurant, Efroyem left Ms. Gibbons' employment. None of the kitchen workers spoke much English, which was fine with Efroyem. What followed that was a succession of low-paying gigs: delivery boy, supermarket cashier, and dog walker. Each of them lasted several years, sometimes a bit longer. He didn't mind any of them, but there never secmed to be a reason to stay. Between these jobs, he fell "back" into hustling. He would return to the bar where he met Kevin or he'd ask Kevin himself if he 'knew anybody that needed anything'. Kevin usually did. But it was always dangerous. One night, two large men awaited Efroyem, and they wouldn't let him leave until they were both done with him.

His "break" came when he found a steady job cleaning the offices at a financial firm downtown. Efroyem worked at night after the workers had gone home for the day. He enjoyed the silence of the work, the darkness outside, and not having to report to anyone. His work was thorough, and he always arrived on time so his supervisor had no reason to question or otherwise engage him. On the rare occasions, when he saw a staff member at the financial firm stay late, Efroyem would say, 'Good evening' to them. Usually, they responded without looking up at him; sometimes they didn't respond at all.

'Isn't it funny, Ma? So much of your day is spent cleaning, and Ta writes *khidushim*/novellae about purity and cleanliness. In a way, I went into the family business.'

Yente smiled at her son's observation but didn't comment. Efroyem grew tired at that point but Yente found that she wasn't ready to leave just yet. She sat with him for several more hours. She wanted to be there in case he woke up. But Efroyem didn't. Yente closed the door behind her on the sounds of his ragged breathing.

***

Early the next morning, she received a telephone call from Summer. Efroyem had passed away during the night. The cremation would take place very shortly. Efroyem wanted his ashes dispersed into the river. Afterwards, a few of his friends would gather in his apartment. He stipulated that there would be no funeral or formal memorial service of any kind.

Yente called Gitl at home and Reb Motl in the yeshiva to let them know about Efroyem's death and the cremation and gathering that would follow. She dreaded making the calls, but she had to. She owed them both that. She started with Gitl because she thought that would be the easier of the two calls. On the phone, Gitl was concerned but distant.

'I'm so sorry to hear that, Ma. How are you?'

'How could I be?'

'I won't be attending the funeral.'

'There won't be a funeral, Gitl. There will be a cremation and then a get-together in Efroyem's apartment.'

'Even in death, he had to have it his way and step all over our *yerushe*. Great, just great.'

'He is your brother, Gitl, and he is no longer with us.'

'Yeah, well, you know … You know what, Ma, thanks for letting me know. That's all I'm gonna say righ' now.'

Reb Motl's response wasn't unexpected.

'He's been dead to me since night a long time. You shouldn't have interrupted my learning. *Bitl-Toyre*. And don't think I didn't know where you've been going all this time. I just wanted to see you if you'd tell me.'

After a long silence, Yente said goodbye and ended the call. She realized that she would have to face the day without the accompaniment of a family member. A living one, that is. Efroyem's spirit would be with her tomorrow and always.

***

Yente met the group at the designated spot on the pier a few hours later. Besides Summer and Steve, there were two men there named Alfred and Franklin. In silence, each of them scooped up some ashes and tossed them into the river. When the urn was passed to her, Yente declined it. She couldn't bring herself to partake in the ritual. As Gitl reminded her (not that she needed reminding), religious law forbade cremation; the dead were to be buried. Yente was horrified by the reduction of her son to ashes. Soot really. Of course, as the mother of the deceased, she wouldn't have been able to wash the body and dress the body. But, after all her involvement in tending the bodies of the recently departed, the reduction of her son's body to ashes was especially bitter. Beyond the personal introductions, there were no other words spoken at the pier, also according to Efroyem's wishes.

Back in Efroyem's studio, Yente busied herself with preparing the food, some of which were leftovers from yesterday. Alfred explained that he dated Efroyem for about a year nearly ten years ago. Franklin met him in a park five years ago, and he and Efroyem remained friends ever since. He didn't elaborate on what exactly transpired during this encounter in the park. When Yente asked Alfred if Efroyem ever explained to him how he'd contracted AIDS, he stared at her disbelief and then said:

'AIDS? Ephraim didn't have AIDS. He died of lung cancer. And he never even smoked. He never told you during your visits?!'

Yente apologized (for what exactly she didn't know) and said:

'No, Efroyem never told me.'

She cast her eyes down and withdrew from the conversation into a bog of questions. The symptoms of AIDS and lung cancer were, of course, so different. Why hadn't she allowed herself to look, to see her son? Why did she assume she knew his illness? Did she believe deep down that it was punishment for the path he embarked on since leaving home? Why didn't she ask? Did she not want to know? Was she afraid to find out? Did she, a *rebetsin* steeped these many years in the demands of inquiry and observation, willfully embrace ignorance?

Shortly thereafter, Alfred and Franklin left together. They knew not to hug Yente. Only Summer and Yente remained. The two of them sat together on Efroyem's bed, with all of his medicine vials nearby. Yente was never able to bring herself to look at their labels. Summer said she wanted to tell Yente about her life with Efroyem.

She met him during the dog walking period of his life. She saw him walking through the square with the dogs and stopped to chat with him. She thought he was cute, adorable really, with his warm eyes that looked not at but into you, wavy brown hair, and lean physique. They spent a lot of time together, even when it became clear very soon thereafter that Efroyem "didn't bat for my team". She had suggestions for him about getting steadier, more "respectable" employment. She regularly let him know about jobs that didn't require a college degree or classes at the community college, especially ones about photography when she found out he took photos in his spare time.

After nearly a year of badgering him to let her see his photographs, Efroyem finally relented. He took her into his studio, which was in a warehouse about forty-five minutes away by train. In his studio were boxes and boxes of photographs of men in a variety of poses and settings. Thousands and thousands of photographs all dated and carefully cataloged. Most were in black and white. Some of the men were handsome, some not so very. Some were nude and indoors; some were fully clothed and on the street or in a restaurant or a park. All of the photographs were distinguished by an intensity, an emotional connection with the photographer. The compositions were exquisitely framed, yet looked naturalistic, casual almost. Efroyem explained to her that all of the models were hustlers. People that Ephraim knew from his own days in the business, and ones he came to know. Some he came to know quite well and love. Sex workers, in today's parlance.

'Here. Let me show you, Mrs. Koplewitz.'

Summer stood up, went to the closet and retrieved a coffee-table sized book with glossy pages from the closet. Its title read *Ephraim Koplewitz: a Retrospective*. Summer explained that it was the catalog of an exhibition she'd curated at her gallery. Yente opened and leafed through it. She saw faces staring back at her. Even the standing nudes looked directly at her. In all of the photos, the men's genitalia were exposed. There were no fig leaves or discreet positioning. Once, years ago, Yente had snuck out to the public library and browsed an art book there. Even with their eyes averted and their sex covered, Yente had felt ashamed for the models that sat for the paintings and photographs. She felt ashamed looking at them. Yes, perhaps that was it. She felt ashamed for herself. Efroyem's work bore no resemblance to those reproductions. His models were not brazen exactly since Efroyem captured them, with tenderness, in their vulnerability and curiosity, and sometimes, matter-of-factness. Their gazes and stances suggested self-acceptance. Here I am. See me here. But perhaps it was her maternal pride taking over. Pride? Yes! How far I've come, she thought. And then: but what do I know about art?

'You should have seen him at the exhibition opening. He was so handsome, so excited. Some of the models came to the opening, and we did a group portrait with the artist. I have that picture at home. I'd never seen him that happy before. I knew he was happy when he was creating his art, when he was photographing the models and working alone in his studio. But I never saw him *that* happy. I tried to get him to continue showing his work after this exhibit, but he refused. Of course, when I found out about his illness, I wondered if it was from the dark room. You know, the chemicals. But maybe it was from all of the smoke he inhaled in the bars? I suppose we'll never know now. But I want you to have a copy of this catalog.'

Summer handed Yente the catalog and the two of them started to clear away the food. Yente packed it up in bags for Summer to take home. A homeless shelter would be coming tomorrow to take away Efroyem's furniture. She, Summer would be packing up Efroyem's clothes and donating them to a thrift shop benefiting people with AIDS. Yente thanked Summer for her friendship with Efroyem, and then, impulsively, hugged her tightly, feeling her slim body steady against what she imagined to her own quivering immensity. As Yente left her son's apartment for the last time, she asked Summer to remain in contact with her. The fragrance of Summer's perfume – something jarringly citrus, bright – remained with her as she descended the now familiar apartment building stairs.

***

Yente walked the streets of Efroyem's neighborhood that night, his exhibition catalog scorching her plaid plastic shopping bag. She wanted to walk the pavement where her son might once have walked. Here, he might have gone to the grocery store; here to purchase vegetables for a salad. What did she know of his eating habits as a grown man?

She remembered how as a little boy he liked to go produce shopping with her. He was drawn by the bright colors – the red and green apples and peppers, the oranges of the fruit and carrots, the yellows of the lemons, the purples of the eggplants.

He loved all of it. He was an artist even then, she thought. Efroyem watched her as she squeezed the fruit, feeling for ripeness. She felt his eyes upon her even when she wasn't looking at him. And when they returned home, they made the salads together. Efroyem couldn't handle a knife at that age, but he liked to watch her peel and cut the fruits and vegetables. And unlike Gitl and so many other children, Efroyem actually liked eating vegetables, loved them, in fact. Even then, her little one had been different, unusual.

The sequence of recent events weighed on her. She knew more about the strangers she visited in hospitals and the dead she tended in the *khevre-kadishe* than the illness and life of her own son. And what she did know seemed to be the result of a string of coincidences. If Tsirl hadn't been with her caring for the dead … If Tsirl hadn't been moved to say something … If Alfred hadn't told her … If Summer hadn't told her … If Efroyem hadn't told her … Only then she thought perhaps these weren't coincidences at all. Perhaps there was a twisting line from the vegetables that Efroyem relished to his leaving the house immediately after Reb Motl ordered him out to his choices of livelihood to his reluctance to show his photographs to Summer to his one exhibition to his illness to his refusing hospice care to his insisting on cremation. Perhaps it had do with his *akshones*. How could she ever know?

But whatever the path of Efroyem's life, *Hashem* led her back to him before it was too late. Even if she couldn't tend to Efroyem as she wanted, even if she couldn't bring herself to ask him about his illness or even look at his medicine vials, even if she never told him "I love you" after he was banished from home that night, even if she couldn't be with him as he parted this world, she did do something. Not enough, she felt, but something. *Hashem* would help her in the days and years to come. She would ask *Hashem* for forgiveness. She would return to the pier that was the closest thing he had to a gravesite and ask Efroyem himself for forgiveness.

Yente took a break from her wanderings. She didn't know where she was or what time of the night it was. She sat on a random stoop and took the exhibition catalog from her shopping bag. But she couldn't bring herself to look through it. She wondered why this volume upset more than the revelations of his work the sex with men, and for money no less. Was it because it was all that was tangible that remained of him? But surely that wasn't it. She had her memories that were surely just as tangible. She would unearth memories of Efroyem when he had been with her at home, when his little hand was clasped in hers as they walked down the avenue, as she adjusted her stride to his. Memories that would be just as bright and colorful as the vegetables Efroyem so savored. She would find them. And she would learn about his life when he had walked out of the house against her pleas. But later. Yes, later. Just as she'd look through these photographs later.

Tonight, she saw her son in his red dark room, breathing in the toxic chemicals, concentrating on his art. Happy. She would nurture that image when sitting next with the dead. She would even somehow find a way to treasure this volume, to see it as other than degrading and filthy. *Tome*. A *tome*, she almost smiled at the word play, despite the occasion. Yes, she was his mother and thus (perhaps) not eligible for washing the dead. But tonight she would sit on this stoop and wash her son of his sorrow. She would clothe him in his shrouds. She would usher his spirit into the world to come. Soon, soon she would find him there. His head at last and truly in the clouds.

"Angel of the Underworld"

A tepid afternoon light filled the *beys-medresh*. It was the sort of day when it wasn't clear whether it was sunny or cloudy, mild or chilly. The gilt bindings of the sacred books that lined the walls and covered the *shtenders* seemed to glow more steadily, more brightly in such ambiguity of light and climate. The scholars, all of them married, were in various poses of study. Some were seated; some were standing. Some were bent over the *shtenders* in concentration, while others gestured passionately. Some even jumped up and down to emphasize a point or an insight only just gleaned from a particularly thorny passage of the Talmud.

Although Meyer had seen and been a participant in this scene and others like it for many years, everything seemed strangely sharper and clearer to him today. Maybe it was because of the weather. Maybe it was because Yerukhem, his *khavruse,* wasn't there. Yerukhem's wife Brokhe was in the hospital about to give birth to their first child. Although he occasionally spotted other scholars "bumming" around in the hallways or the coatroom or sometimes even in the *beys-medresh* itself, Meyer rarely joined them. Nor was he prone to bouts of looking around the room. As a rule, Meyer tried to stay focused on the text under scrutiny. His time here was precious, and he didn't want anything to distract him from learning.

His wife Feygi wouldn't have wanted that, either. Meyer considered himself fortunate that Feygi supported his Torah study both financially and emotionally. Feygi was a manager in a supermarket a few blocks off the main shopping avenue. Her father also provided additional financial support during the holidays or when the occasion warranted it. Feygi never complained about the meager stipend that the *kolel* paid Meyer.

Of course, Yerukhem wouldn't have allowed Meyer's attention to stray far from their study. Yerukhem was renowned through the *kolel* for his ability to comprehend a difficult text and to extricate layers of meaning with great speed. His originality of thought coupled with his profound humility (a rare combination) endeared him to his teachers from an early age. Recently, just several years into *kolel* study, Yerukhem published a volume of original commentaries on the tractate Sukkah fronted by five letters of rabbinical approbation. Yerukhem intended to remove his name from the volume, but Meyer convinced him otherwise. Why shouldn't people know these were his insights? Besides, Meyer was proud of Yerukhem's accomplishments and wanted others to know of them, too. Meyer donated a small amount and helped gather the funds to finance publication. When Yerukhem gave him a copy of the volume, Meyer turned to the preface and was pleased to see that Yerukhem had thanked him profusely for his contributions in the acknowledgments. The handwritten inscription on the flyleaf was more understated but no less heartfelt: 'To my partner in learning, to my friend, Meyer, with thanks always, Yerukhem.' He made sure to convey his own thanks to Yerukhem for both the mention and the inscription.

Meyer was surprised when Yerukhem agreed to be his *khavruse*. He could easily have selected any of the most outstanding young men in the *kolel*. Meyer heard that Yerukhem's previous *khavruse* was leaving the *kolel* to go into business with his father-in-law and wasted no time in asking him. An electronics store was the previous *khavruse*'s new line of business, if Meyer wasn't mistaken. Maybe it was just a matter of timing, of being the first to ask Yerukhem. Maybe Yerukhem took pity on him, Meyer sometimes thought. Meyer's father died of an unexpected heart attack at age fifty-three, a month and a half before Meyer became a bar mitzvah. Meyer was in a period of intense preparation with his father for his *pshetil*, regularly fine-tuning it with his father's guidance. One day his mother had found his father bent over his *shtender* and broke the news to Meyer when he came from yeshiva.

Still, if timing or pity had landed him Yerukhem's *khavruse*-ship, they alone could not have guaranteed its continuity and success. Meyer found himself rising to the occasion. He prepared at home every evening, readying himself for Yerukhem's probing questions the next day. He reviewed not only the page of the Talmud but also Rashi and Toysfes as well as some of the more advanced commentaries if time permitted.

Meyer prepared with similar focus and intensity after his father's death. Arguably, this was when he really developed the discipline to become a Torah scholar. His mother didn't allow him to buckle under the grief. After the funeral and the mourning period, which Meyer now remembered as a wash of grief and gray, his mother came into his room and told him he had to go on. He had to go back to yeshiva and continue his preparations for his bar mitzvah. This is what his father would have wanted for him. Even as she plunged into the preparation of the vast amount of food for the celebration, his mother kept Meyer on track. Meyer could hardly recall his father's voice now and sometimes wondered if he would recall his face if his mother hadn't placed photographs discreetly yet strategically around their apartment, such as on bookcases, end tables, and in the dining room breakfront.

During the period after his father's death, Meyer studied every night until exhaustion in the dining room beneath the portraits of rabbinical sages who influenced his father. The portrait of Reb Hirsh, the head of his father's yeshiva, who was still living and delivered the eulogy at his funeral, was enlarged and hung above his father's now empty seat at the table. When Meyer was seven years old, his father brought him on the eve of Yom Kippur to Reb Hirsh for a blessing. He remembered Reb Hirsh's kindly face and the touch of his hands on his head, if not the words of the blessing itself. Perhaps it was the long-ago blessing given by Reb Hirsh that helped him become who he was today. Reb Hirsh sat at the table next to him during his bar mitzvah festivities. While delivering his *pshetil*, Meyer looked out at the room and saw his mother standing with the women in the back (in the next room actually), beaming with pride. Reb

Hirsh was the first to offer him *yasher-koyekh* after he completed the *pshetil* without error.

As Meyer looked around the *beys-medresh*, his mind wandered to Yerukhem and Brokhe. He hoped all was well but he didn't want to reach out to them at this point. Not just yet. Let Yerukhem and Brokhe spend this time together. It was a special time for them, when they would fulfill the biblical commandment to be fruitful and multiply, when they would be blessed with a source of *nakhes* for themselves, when they could bring a new member into the House of Israel.

Meyer and Feygi had tried without success for more than three years to conceive. It wasn't easy for Meyer to fulfill his duties as a husband. He'd known for years that he was burdened with unwanted same sex attraction. It started at puberty and never relented. He was always careful never to let anyone know or suspect, keeping his eyes averted in the locker room or elsewhere. It was especially hard in the yeshiva dormitory, but he managed by taking a shower very early in the morning. Fortunately, the yeshiva showers had not been communal.

When he was in bed with Feygi, Meyer found the images of handsome men coming into his mind – men he saw on the street or the rare occasions when he rode the subway or even in the *beys-medresh* itself. He didn't exactly welcome them, but neither did he banish them. As much as he tried not to, he sometimes even thought of Yerukhem himself when he was in bed with Feygi. Besides his intellect, Yerukhem was gifted with a fine physique broad shoulders, muscular chest, slim waist and a handsome face illuminated by penetrating hazel eyes. Despite the many hours they spent together each week, Meyer trained his eyes to look away from Yerukhem's physical self and to focus instead on the texts in front of them. But sometimes just hearing Yerukhem's voice excited Meyer. Somehow Meyer was able to consummate his marriage, even as he knew that Feygi must surely have suspected that the desire wasn't there on his part. He hoped Feygi didn't attribute his performance to her own shortcomings, and he tried to be especially attentive to her during their time together outside the marital bed.

Still, Meyer could tell by the sidelong glances that Feygi gave him when she thought he wouldn't notice or by the sighs that seemed to inadvertently escape from her that she knew quite well who he was and what he wasn't giving her. In fact, Meyer detected just such a glance and sigh this morning when she was sipping her coffee standing at the kitchen sink, her slim figure piercing the indeterminate light, while he was seated at the table eating his granola with bananas. His thoughts flicked lazily from the water in the dishpan to the gray of Feygi's housecoat to the light outside. Could light be dishwashy, he asked himself.

But more pointedly, Meyer couldn't help but notice that even in a frayed housecoat Feygi somehow maintained a certain elegance. Meyer wondered if the housecoat itself was a sign. Growing up, his mother had never worn such a garment in the kitchen, even at the beginning of the day. It seemed to Meyer that Feygi's unhappiness didn't stem merely from their childlessness as a couple or even from her dissatisfaction with his "present absence" in the night chamber, but rather from a deeper, essential lack in Meyer himself. Meyer thought back to their few "dates" in a restaurant after their match had been made by a neighborhood rebetsin. Their conversation often faltered, despite their shared objective of raising a large, Torah-observant family. Even then Feygi had been quiet (perhaps furtive?), loath to make full eye contact yet somehow not missing anything. Had Feygi known even then about him? If so, why had she agreed to marry him? Of course, he could never bring himself to ask her.

Meyer wondered for years whether his attraction to men would prevent him from getting married. When his mother spoke with him about a matchmaker who was investigating possible matches for him, Meyer made an appointment to visit Reb Hirsh. Although he'd seldom seen him since his bar mitzvah, Meyer felt that Reb Hirsh could guide him. Reb Hirsh's *talmed muvhek* who functioned as his assistant, ushered Meyer into Reb Hirsh's book-lined study. Reb Hirsh welcomed him and immediately launched into an analysis of the Talmudic tractate he was then studying (*Bava kama*). As their discussion deepened, Meyer wondered how exactly he would bring up the cause of his visit. Only he didn't have to. Reb Hirsh asked Meyer about his marriage plans. Meyer thought carefully beforehand about how he was going to speak about this matter with Reb Hirsh.

'Rebe, I actually came to speak with you about that *inyen*. This is hard for me to talk about, and I haven't told anyone else about it. I've been attracted to men all my adult life. I've tried to stop these thoughts, but I can't. They never go away. I don't know if I can be *mekayem* my *khiyev* with a woman. Does the Rebe think I should get married?'

Reb Hirsh didn't seem shocked or even surprised by Meyer's revelation. He looked down briefly and then replied:

'I'm glad you told me about this, Meyer. *Her zikh ayn*, we all have the *yeytser-hore* inside of us. Everyone faces challenges to remaining on the *derekh ha-yosher* of the Torah and *Khazal*. This *tayve* just happens to be your challenge. You have to work hard, harder than you've been working, to overcome what the *yeytser-hore* has set in front of you. You must get married and be *mekayem* the mitzvah of *peru u-revu*. Don't separate yourself from *Klal Yisroel*. And don't forget that you are a *ben yokhed*. It's your responsibility to carry on the name of your father. Think of your mother. Think of how much *nakhes* she will get from you as a father and from grandchildren!'

Both of them looked down and fell into silence following Reb Hirsh's response. There didn't seem to be anything else to add. Nothing Reb Hirsh said was new to him. After what seemed like an appropriate interval, Meyer thanked Reb Hirsh for his guidance, shook his hand, and left, this time without the accompaniment of the *talmed muvhek*. Even if his burden hadn't exactly been lifted, Meyer was relieved to have shared it with someone.

As he left Reb Hirsh's office, Meyer found himself wondering (not for the first time) if would he have "developed" differently if his father hadn't died at that crucial point in his life. This conjecture arose from a magazine article he came across in the dentist's office shortly after his father's death. The article stated that homosexuality in males was the result of an "overbearing" mother and a distant father. He remembered shuddering back then while reading it, hoping his mother wouldn't notice. And buried in her Psalms, she didn't. Even if she did notice, his mother probably would have attributed it to his dentist-waiting-room-nerves. Of course, Meyer now knew that that this once reigning theory had long been categorically discredited by all reputable scientists. And yet he was also quite aware that there were entire programs dedicated to "changing" the desires of those like him. He'd seen their advertisements discreetly placed in various communal publications. Meyer was grateful to Reb Hirsh for not suggesting such a program.

After several dates with Feygi (one at a Chinese restaurant, the other a walk in the park the next neighborhood over), Meyer considered telling her about his "condition". But he really was enjoying her company, and he felt drawn to her slim figure and grace, her way of listening to his words as if they were of great importance. He felt that he had the potential to build a God-fearing home with Feygi. He didn't want to scare her away and ruin his chances. Two other young women had already rejected him. It really was time to settle down. When he was walking down the wedding aisle, his arm linked in his mother's, he wondered again whether he should have revealed his secret to Feygi. As she completed her seven circles around him under the *khupe* and stood by his side, Meyer understood that it was too late. He would now never reveal this part of himself to Feygi.

As his mind continued to drift in Yerukhem's absence, Meyer decided to step away from the *beys-medresh*. It was nearly lunchtime in any case. Grabbing his jacket but leaving his fedora in the coatroom, Meyer left without informing anyone. He walked briskly towards the subway station and descended the station. Sometimes Meyer thought of the descent into the subway station as his descent into the underworld, into *Gehenem* itself. Here commenced the voyage that would take him into the heart of what he simultaneously desired and what he desired to avoid.

***

The theater auditorium was dark, with little illumination from the scene onscreen. Meyer waited briefly against the wall to allow his eyes to adjust to the darkness before making his way to a seat in the back. He had little experience with theaters since movies, with their incitement of lust and their overall frivolity, were forbidden in the community.

But Meyer had been coming regularly to this theater and several others like it for several years, nearly immediately after his marriage. He came at times of the day when he imagined himself to be least conspicuous late afternoon or after dinner, when he was supposed to be at his *seyder*. It only took about a half-hour each way to reach the area in the city where the theaters were located. If he were careful, the entire excursion could last no more than two and a half hours, sometimes considerably less. Meyer found such visits considerably less risky than purchasing magazines from the kiosk. He really had nowhere safe to hide them. A locked desk drawer in his study might have aroused Feygi's suspicion when she came in to clean.

Meyer was in the neighborhood to visit the central library when he first happened upon on this theater. Yerukhem had asked him to examine an early edition of a commentary, printed in Vienna towards the end of the nineteenth century, of which only eight copies were known to be extant. Yerukhem's insistence was well-placed. Meyer found the edition to be rich with insightful glossa handwritten by another commentator who was clearly not the author. He wondered if Yerukhem had informed the librarian of the treasure but decided not to approach him. He'd ask Yerukhem later. Buoyed by this encounter with a rare text and glossa, Meyer decided to walk around the neighborhood before returning home. After several blocks, he noticed the proliferation of theaters with flashing white and red lights. Most had the outlines of the female form above their door. However, on a side street just off the main avenue, Meyer spotted one with a male silhouette and a sign that read "Adonis" above its door. Meyer felt his heart begin to race and quickly paid the entrance fee. Just like that, without thinking it through.

The smell in the theater was both stale and sharp. There was a sour human odor that could not be eradicated by a regularly applied overlay of industrial-strength cleaning fluid. Meyer entered the auditorium and looked at the film onscreen. He realized that, with his fedora, beard, and long black coat, he was conspicuous even in the dark theater. Meyer's eyes drifted from the images onscreen to the movement in the theater itself. Individual men stood in the theater aisles before finding companions who were already seated. Sometimes they sat with them for a long time, embracing, groping, stroking, even sucking. Meyer could hear the slurping and gagging sounds. He could see that the seated theatergoers who had their crotches completely exposed and their pants on the floor were the most likely to invite company. Meyer kept his pants on, not wishing to attract any company in the seats next to him. When a fellatio scene onscreen struck him as particularly pleasing, he reached efficient release and exited the theater. He reached for a paper towel that he always kept in his pocket. You just never know when you'll need it …

Meyer had come a long way since that first time. He stopped wearing his fedora and suit jacket here. He put his yarmulke in his pocket and kept his *tsitses* underneath his pants, instead of outside them or in his pockets as he typically wore them. He rarely sought the company of any of the theatergoers, although sometimes he allowed one of them to stroke him to orgasm. Meyer never tried to excuse this activity to himself. He understood that what he was doing was proscribed and prayed he would one day, somehow through divine intervention, be freed from this demon.

Thinking of Yerukhem and Brokhe in the hospital, Meyer found a seat in the middle of the auditorium. His eyes drifted lazily to the scene onscreen. There wasn't much happening – a square-jawed man was driving a pickup truck through the desert. Meyer felt a presence beside him and a hand rest on his thigh. He allowed half a minute to elapse before turning his head slightly. A young man, in his early twenties, perhaps just a few years younger than himself, smiled at him, radiant in the dark. Meyer smiled in return and felt the young man's hands travel ever so slightly up and then down his thigh. Meyer was surprised when the young man's hand didn't reach for his groin. Instead, when he turned to him, the young man moved his face closer and began to kiss Meyer. Meyer turned his head more fully to him, ran his hands over his shirt covering a lean upper body, and moved his tongue deep inside the young man's mouth. When they stopped to take a break, the credits for the film rolled up the screen. Meyer realized he had to get home. He smiled and introduced himself to the young man, who introduced himself as Silas. As he stood up to go, the young man gestured for him to wait. He found a scrap of paper in his wallet, wrote down his name and number and handed it to Meyer, who thanked him. He pocketed the piece of paper and hurried out of the theater.

***

Several days later, the good news arrived. Brokhe gave birth to a baby girl; both mother and child were in good health. Yerukhem, Brokhe, and their families were relieved the birth had not needed to be a Caesarian as feared. Yerukhem had remained with Brokhe in the delivery room throughout the birthing process. Back in the *beys-medresh*, Yerukhem was surrounded by well-wishers and greeted everywhere with "Mazl tov!" and handshakes. Throughout their *sedorim*, they were exuberantly interrupted by congratulations for Yerukhem. When the fifth group of well-wishers left, Meyer found it difficult to refocus his attention on their study and asked Yerukhem about their plans for the upcoming *kidesh* for the baby. He knew Feygi was baking a *lokshn kugl* and a chocolate cake, but did they need anything else? As Meyer listened to Yerukhem's plans, he wondered if his own carefully crafted home life was going to unravel just as Yerukhem's was becoming fully anchored.

The scrap of yellow paper, with the name and phone number blazed in his wallet. Meyer found himself thinking repeatedly about the young man from the theater. Meyer had never heard of the name "Silas" before. What kind of name was it? One afternoon, he slipped into a telephone booth on the avenue and called him. He was about to leave a message (without his number) on the answering machine when Silas answered the phone.

'Hello. Is this Silas? Oh good, this is Meyer. M-e-y-e-r. We met several weeks ago at the theater in the city. Yes … yeah, that was me. Um … I was wondering if you'd like to meet some time for coffee some time. Maybe late afternoon?'

'Sure, I'd love to. I'm free any evening this week. How about Thursday?'

'Um … Yes, I can make it on Thursday.'

'Great! There's a café downtown that had comfortable sofas and chairs in separate groupings for privacy. Would that work for you, Meyer?'

'Sure.'

'Do you know where it is?'

'No, but I'm sure I'll find it if you give me the address, Silas.'

'It's at … Great, well, I look forward to meeting you there.'

'Same here! Take care, Silas.'

When he hung up the telephone, Meyer was pleased that he wouldn't have to think up an excuse. The meeting – no, the date – would be between his afternoon *seyder* and supper. He'd be able to meet Silas and be back at home in time for supper. There, he'd done it. With that rather ordinary conversational exchange, he had arranged his first date with a man. The fork in the road that he reached when he entered the Adonis Theater was branching out, or forking, yet again. Was Meyer now officially off the *derekh*?

***

Silas looked even more appealing in the lamplight of the café. His light brown hair was neatly combed, not long exactly, but not a crew cut, either. He stood up and smiled at Meyer, hugging him and asking him if he wanted to order anything. Meyer declined but accepted a glass of water when the waitress came by to take their order. Silas ordered a slice of white chocolate mousse cake. As the waitress left their seating area, Meyer glanced around the café and noticed men sitting with other men, and women sitting with women. He'd heard of gay bars, of course, but were there also gay cafes?

Silas now worked at a gay bar in the evenings, having just quit his job at a health foods cafe. He'd moved from the country to the city only a year ago. When he first moved to the city, he lived at the YMCA and had just moved to a studio apartment about a half hour from this café, in fact. The name "Silas" was probably a shortened form of the name "Silvanus", a companion of Saint Paul in the New Testament. Another interpretation was that it was a Greek form of the Hebrew name "Sha'ul".

'Do you have any opinion on this debate?' Silas asked with a smile.

'No. And I must confess that I'm not very knowledgeable about the New Testament and have only a smattering of Ancient Greek.'

He wasn't sure what to share exactly about himself. He'd never met anyone in a social, let alone erotic/romantic situation that didn't know anything about him. Meyer decided therefore to be totally upfront. He said:

'I'm a scholar of the Talmud and rabbinical literature. I'm married without children.'

'I'm surprised to hear you're married. I didn't see a ring on your fingers in the theater and don't see one now. Did you take it off?'

'The men in my community don't wear wedding rings; they're for women only. The husband says to his betrothed: "With this ring you are consecrated to me."'

Meyer tried to speak in a lively tone, hoping he didn't sound too teacherly or pedantic to Silas. But Silas appeared attentive throughout, asking pointed questions about his community and keeping the conversation going. After about an hour, when Meyer glanced at his watch, he realized (again) he had to return home. The two made plans to meet the following week.

***

The baby's name was Miryem-Zisl, Miryem after Brokhe's maternal grandmother and Zisl after Yerukhem's paternal grandmother. The *kidesh* in her honor was well attended, overflowing even. The men sat on long tables in the living room, and the women stood packed in the dining room near the kitchen. Meyer made sure to sample Feygi's *lokshn kugl* and chocolate cake. He would compliment her on both when they got home. Yerukhem gave a brief speech, thanking all of those in attendance for their support and good wishes and sang the praises of Brokhe, his one-and-only and a true woman of valor. As the celebration unfolded, Meyer thought about how he could bring it to life for Silas at their next get-together. What details would be the most telling? The sentiments of Yerukhem's speech? The food? The singing? His own happiness for Yerukhem and Brokhe laced with longing (envy?)? No, not that. Of course, not that. The two had already seen each other several times, and Meyer was looking forward to seeing him again, even if he still wasn't comfortable with the word "date".

That get-together arrived sooner than Meyer expected. Silas lived on a noisy street, with music blaring from windows and children playing in the street. Meyer opened a squeaky metal door and climbed some metal stairs, hearing the sounds of babies crying, and presented Silas with a bouquet of red roses he purchased in a kiosk near the subway station. Silas' apartment was narrow, with each room leading into the other, "railroad" style.

The table was set; Silas said he wanted to surprise Meyer.

'I know you have to get back home soon, but I wanted to cook you a meal, chicken and green beans. It's the favorite meal my grandmother used to make for me. My grandmother – Gran raised him from when I was little. I still call her twice a week. She's doing good. Gosh, I'm talking too much.'

'No you're not, Silas. I want to learn about you.'

Gran's picture stood on a table beneath a mirror near the front door to Silas' apartment. When Silas saw Meyer looking over at her picture and then the statue of Jesus that stood next to the picture, he said:

'Gran just sent me that Jesus. I used to go to church with her every Sunday. Anyhow, let's eat.'

Meyer tried to conceal his panic. He'd planned their get-togethers so carefully until today. And now this. A non-kosher meal in an apartment with a *getshke* with a man *nisht fun di eygene*. What was he doing here? Just one of these variables wouldn't have been so egregious, but each seemed to build on the other, creating a tower of transgression.

He wanted to tell Silas that he couldn't eat this food even if it looked delicious, that he kept kosher. Maybe it was the smooth skin peering out from Silas' shirt or his slightly flushed face or all the trouble he had gone to in preparing the dinner but Meyer couldn't refuse him. In any case, he could see that there was no pork or anything obviously *treyf* on the table. It would have to be okay tonight. Meyer would ask God to forgive him yet another trespass. He sat down and devoured Silas' meal and complimented him on his cooking skills, ones that he lacked entirely. Meyer's mother, the cook in the yeshiva, and then Feygi cooked all his meals. Meyer had done little more in the kitchen than prepare scrambled eggs or a tuna fish salad sandwich.

After dinner, Silas led Meyer to the couch, and the two began to kiss. Silas unbuttoned Meyer's shirt and began to lick his chest and nipples. He led Meyer to his bedroom, the windowless middle one in the railroad apartment and stripped, glowing in the light of dusk. He stood before Meyer fully erect. Except for his pubes and underarms, Silas' body was mostly hairless, so unlike Meyer's own. Meyer quickly followed his example and placed his clothes on the chair next to his bed. Silas placed a lubricated condom on Meyer (just in case!), lay on his stomach on the bed, and opened his legs.

As Meyer entered Silas, it occurred to him how different this was from his entering Feygi. On this night, the goal was to prevent the semen from swimming out; on all other nights, its dissemination (!!) was eagerly sought. After a brief clenching, Silas rose to meet Meyer's thrusts. The two found a rhythm; Meyer felt himself expanding into Silas. As Meyer wrapped his arms around him, finding his points of pleasure, Silas moaned. Meyer felt that this was where he belonged, where he was meant to be. When he came shortly after Silas, he stayed on top on him, his cock resting between Silas' ass cheeks. The two lay like that until their breath was restored to evenness.

Meyer was awakened by the quiet. The boom boxes had gone silent. Children were no longer playing on the pavement. Meyer didn't want to awaken Silas, who was snoring lightly in his arms. He extricated himself gently from Silas' arms and quickly dressed. He left a note on Silas' front table next to the portrait of Gran and the statue of Jesus, stating simply, 'Thank you!' and left.

On the subway ride back home, Meyer considered the sins he'd committed in just one evening, the pleasures of forbidden food and flesh that he'd savored. He wondered how he would get right by *Hashem*; surely, the accounts against him were stacking up in the divine ledger. What would he pray for next Yom Kippur? How could he so blithely betray the memory of his father and the dreams of his mother who lifted him from his grief after his father's death to become a Torah scholar?

And yet as the train went underground, Meyer observed his smiling reflection in the window. To be sure, he was not smiling as widely as Silas when he saw Meyer standing in his doorway with a bouquet of red roses, but he was smiling nonetheless. He thought of Silas leaving his grandmother to live in the city. He thought of the miracle of Silas finding him in the theater auditorium, with its groping and sticky floors and industrial-strength cleanser. Meyer wished he could share the news of Silas with Yerukhem or Reb Hirsh or his mother, if not Feygi. He wondered if he would have the strength to leave the world he'd always known as Silas did, if their life trajectories would ever parallel each other or even converge. He wondered if his mother would continue to speak to him, as Silas' grandmother still spoke to him, if he ever did leave the community. He thought about the sins he committed, which somehow didn't feel like sins. Meyer thought of Silas's smile, of his light brown curls, of his hand on his thigh, of his slim body opening to him. And the word "sin" didn't feel right, or even relevant here.

As he walked up to the door of his apartment building, Meyer didn't feel that he was returning from the underworld as he usually did when returning from the theater. He had been in light, and would now continue to be in light. The duality in which he had lived all of his adult life had somehow taken a turn. The dialectic between dream and reality had been bridged. With the touch of Silas still tingling on his skin, he was a different man somehow. For all the transgressions committed, he was tonight the man he needed to be. Soon he would see Feygi in their marital bed, her breath rising in slumber (or feigned

172

slumber). Tomorrow he would be with Yerukhem, the excitement of the birth of Miryem-Zisl having leveled off. They would continue in their study of the Talmudic tractate *Sukkah*, and Meyer's eyes would not be averted from his *khavruse*. His joy would meet Yerukhem's.

As Meyer unlocked the door, he thought of the three people of his generation who were closest to him and the web of knowing and not-knowing that connected them all, and he was filled with an almost overwhelming sense of affection for and well-being in the world. And he thought too of his mother, whose image receded somewhat since he first met Silas. He thought of how overjoyed his mother had been at his choice of Feygi as a bride, how she approved of Feygi's modesty and steadfastness, and of the deep affection that remained between the two of them since the wedding. As Meyer closed the door stealthily behind himself, he took pleasure in the quiet only broken by the refrigerator's melody and the occasional rattling of pipes. His elation still undiminished, Meyer sat on the sofa in the dark and wondered how those connections, threads really, would be reconfigured in these rooms and beyond. Humming soundlessly, he entered their bedroom where Feygi (really) was fast asleep in her bed, the two twisted strands of her white *tikhl* spread against the linen like arms extended in welcome.

A Note on the Transliteration and Pronunciation

For the most part, the transliteration of names in this collection follows Beider, Alexander. *A Dictionary of Ashkenazic Given Names: Their Origins, Structure, Pronunciation, and Migrations* (Bergenfield, N.J.: Avotaynu, 2001). The final "e" in transliterated Yiddish names (e.g. Khane, Sore, Shiye, and Yente) is pronounced "eh", not as in the hard Canadian interrogative "Eh?" but close to the French definite article "le" or the "eah" as in "So what?" or "Big deal!" The final "e" in Mame and Tate are pronounced the same way (e.g. Mameh and Tateh) and NOT like the Mame in "Auntie Mame" or the Tate in "Tate Gallery." Instead of Rokhl, I've transliterated the name as Rahel in "Lettering and the Art of Living" to convey a modern Orthodox sensibility, less connected to theYiddish-speaking realm.

Yiddish words and phrases follow the system of transliteration established by the YIVO Institute of Jewish Research. Most of the words and phrases in this book are of Hebrew origin but accepted into Yiddish. For the sake of consistency, I generally transliterated such words as Yiddish words. For example, I transliterated the *Commentators' Bible* Yiddishly as *Mikroyes gedoyles* and not Hebraically as *Miḳra'ot gedolot*. My transliteration standards for such words are Weinreich, Uriel. *Modern English-Yiddish Yiddish-English Dictonary* (New York: YIVO Institute for Jewish Research, McGraw-Hill Book Company, 1968) and Niborski, Yitskhok. *Verterbukh fun loshn-koydesh shtamike verter in Yidish* (Medem-Bibliotek, 2012).

Words accepted into English, such as Shabbas, Torah, yeshiva, are used according to the spelling in Webster's Dictionary and not as Shabes, Toyre, or yeshive as they would be transliterated in the YIVO system.

Glossary of Hebrew and Yiddish Terms

akshones: obstinacy, persistence
akshonim: plural of akshn, stubborn/obstinate ones
al tarbeh siḥah 'im ishah: Make not plentiful conversation with wom
Am-Haseyfer: the People of the Book
bal tashkhes: prohibition against waste or needless destruction
bekher: wine goblet
ben yokhed: only child
beys-medresh: house of study
Beys-Yankev: also known as Bais Yaakov ("House of Jacob"), a common name for an all-girls religious school
bitl-Toyre: a waste of Torah-learning time, taking someone away from Torah learning
Bney-Yisroel: the People of Israel, the Israelites
bobe, bobi: grandmother
brukhim ha-boim: Welcome
derekh ha-yosher: the path of righteousness
devar Torah: an explication of a Torah passage
emune: faith in God
erev-Shvues: the eve of Pentecost
erlekhe mishpokhe: an upstanding family
Es past nisht: It's not appropriate
Eyn-Yankev: collection of Talmudic legends
farfoylt: rotten
gehenem: hell
gemakh: charity thrift shop
gemitlekh: cozy
getshke: idol

Got vet helfn: God will help

ha-Kodesh Borekh Hu: The Holy One Blessed Be He

ha-Moytse: the breaking of bread

halakhic: pertaining to halakhah, Jewish law

Hashem: literally "the Name", meaning God

hasmodeh: diligence

Her zikh ayn: listen up

Im yirtseshem bay dir: With God's will, for you, too

inyen: matter

ish tam yoshev oholim (Genesis 25:27): a pure man who dwells in tents (in contrast to an outdoorsman)

kavone: special concentration, as in prayer

khavruse: study partner

Khazal: the Sages of blessed memory

khevre kadishe: burial society

kheyder: religious school

khupe: wedding canopy

Kidesh: prayer over wine; communal celebration in a synagogue after Sabbath morning prayers

Klal Yisroel: the Jewish people

kolel: institute for advanced study for married men

limudey-koydesh: religious studies

lokshn kugel: noodle loaf or pudding

mekayem my khiyev: fulfill my requirement

mesivte: Orthodox Jewish yeshiva secondary school for boys

mevaker holim: to visit the sick

mides: character traits

Mikroyes Gedoyles: Commentators' Bible

minkhe: afternoon prayer service

mikve: ritual bath

moyredik: awe-inspiring

nakhes: parental pride and joy

nisht fun di eygene: not of his own kind

peru u-revu: be fruitful and multiply

a por petsh: a few spanks

pshetil: speech

Rashi: Rabbi Shlomo Yitzchaki, 1040-1105, commentator on the Tanakh and the Talmud rebetsin: rabbi's wife

rebi: teacher

Rosh Hashana: the Jewish new year

seyder: study hall

shadkhonim: matchmakers

Shmoys: biblical book of Exodus

shier-khizek: inspirational sermon

Shir ha-maalot mi-maamakim keratikha Adonai: A song of ascent, out of the depths I have called out to thee, O Lord (Psalms 130:1)

Sholesh Regolim: the Pilgrimage Festivals of Tabernacles, Passover, and Pentecost

shmates: rags

shtender: book stand

Shvues: Pentecost, the holiday celebrating the receipt of the Ten Commandments

simkhes: joyous occasions

talmed muvhek: lead student

talmidey-khakhomim: sages

Tate, Tati: father

Tate-mame: father and mother

tayve: lust

tefilin: phylacteries

tikhl: head kerchief worn by married women

tome: ritually impure

Toysfes: medieval commentaries on the Talmud

tsadek: pious/saintly man

tsedeykes: pious/saintly woman

tsholnt: stew eaten on the Sabbath

tome: impure

treyf: non-kosher

tsitses: ritual fringes

vayter: continue, keep going

vort: literally "word", engagement party

yasher-koyekh: congratulations! Well done!

yerushe: heritage

yeytser-hore: the evil inclination

yinglekh: boys